KNOCK ABOUT WITH THE FITZGERALD-TROUTS

KNOCK ABOUT WITH THE FITZGERALD-TROUTS

ESTA SPALDING

illustrated by

SYDNEY SMITH

Little, Brown and Company
New York Boston

Copyright © 2017 by Esta Spalding
Illustrations copyright © 2017 by Sydney Smith

Cover design by Sasha Illingworth/Angela Taldone.
Cover illustration copyright © 2017 by Sydney Smith.
Cover copyright © 2017 by Hachette Book Group, Inc.

Little, Brown and Company
Hachette Book Group
1290 Avenue of the Americas, New York, NY 10104
Visit us at lb-kids.com

First Edition: May 2017

Little, Brown and Company is a division of Hachette Book Group, Inc. The Little, Brown name and logo are trademarks of Hachette Book Group, Inc.

Library of Congress Cataloging-in-Publication Data
Names: Spalding, Esta, author.
Title: Knock about with the Fitzgerald-Trouts / by Esta Spalding.
Description: First edition. | New York ; Boston : Little, Brown and Company, 2017. | Summary: "The Fitzgerald-Trouts must find a new place to live, while they try to protect their island from a nefarious plot masterminded by their terrible father, Johnny Trout"—Provided by publisher.
Identifiers: LCCN 2016019844| ISBN 9780316298605 (hardcover) | ISBN 9780316298612 (ebook) | ISBN 9780316298636 (library edition ebook)
Subjects: | CYAC: Homeless persons—Fiction. | Brothers and sisters—Fiction. | Family life—Fiction. | Plants—Fiction. | Islands—Fiction.
Classification: LCC PZ7.1.S713 Kno 2017 | DDC [Fic]—dc23
LC record available at https://lccn.loc.gov/2016019844

ISBNs: 978-0-316-29860-5 (hardcover), 978-0-316-29861-2 (ebook)

Printed in the United States of America

LSC-C

10 9 8 7 6 5 4 3 2 1

For Annetta Kinnicutt

KNOCK ABOUT WITH THE FITZGERALD-TROUTS

AUTHOR'S NOTE

In early June of last year, I was kayaking home from a visit with my (then) friend Johnny Trout at his cabin on Wabo Point when my boat was attacked by an animal that I can only guess was a giant squid. The last thing I remember was seeing five enormous, fleshy white tentacles (covered with pulsing suckers, each one as big as a toilet plunger) reaching up out of the waves and latching on to the bow of my boat. I turned my head from the sight only to find myself looking into the eye of the terrible beast as it rose up out of the water. It was an eye so large that I saw in it my own life-size reflection— upside down—and for a moment it seemed as if the animal had already swallowed me whole.

I must have lost consciousness because I remember nothing else. I've been told that I was found some hours later, floating faceup in my life jacket in the harbor, and that I remained unconscious for several weeks, in a hospital bed, hovering between life and death.

It was during this time of unconsciousness that the events described in this book took place. I have pieced them together based on the accounts given to me by the four oldest Fitzgerald-Trout children, and I have confirmed what they told me by talking to as many other witnesses as I can find. But I have been warned by my lawyers that if this book is going to be published, I must make clear from the start that the events I am describing— including the criminal activities that Kim, Kimo, Pippa, and Toby swear they witnessed—have not yet been heard in our island's courts by a judge or a jury. In other words, the actual ownership of the boat in question has not yet been decided, and the Fitzgerald-Trout children may, in fact, be the ones on the wrong side of the law. But I don't think so. I think I know whose story to trust.

—E. S.

CHAPTER
1

Kim Fitzgerald-Trout might have been only eleven years old, but she was a very experienced driver, so as she turned onto the road that descended the dark slopes of Mount Muldoon, she slowed her little green car. Her four brothers and sisters were laughing into the darkness around her, repeating lines from the movie they'd just seen at the drive-in. It was only the first week of summer vacation but they had already been to the drive-in twice, which meant that Kim had driven the same road only a few nights before. Still, she drove carefully. The road was surrounded on all sides by a forest of maha trees. Kim didn't want to risk an accident in the battered old car whose engine made a gurgling noise even when it wasn't driving down the steepest mountain on the island.

Kim's brother Kimo, who was the second oldest and sat beside her in the front of the car, saw her fingers clenched on the steering wheel. He nudged her gently with his shoulder, his way of asking if everything was all right. "It's too dark," Kim answered, flicking on the high beams that illuminated more of the road.

"Well done," Kimo said in a phony English accent, and they all laughed appreciatively. It was a line from the movie they had just seen called *The Nosy Ninja*, about a basset-hound ninja who solved crimes by sniffing out the villains. At the end of the movie, the nosy ninja had discovered the stolen diamonds stuffed into a rump roast being overcooked in an oven. That's when the police inspector had patted him on the head and said, "Well done, nosy ninja. Just like this rump roast."

Pippa, who was eight years old and sat in the backseat behind Kimo, shook her fist in the air and repeated the villain's last line from the movie: "You oughta mind your own business, nosy ninja."

"The nose knows," Toby, the second youngest, said, making a sniffing noise just like the basset hound, then pretending first to smell the jar that held his goldfish and then the bald head of Penny, his baby sister, who sat beside him in her car seat.

Penny cooed gleefully, letting loose a slurry of spit-up onto her doll, Lani.

Most children, when they leave a drive-in movie theater, go home and get in their beds and go to sleep, but the Fitzgerald-Trouts were not most children. When they left the drive-in, they stayed in their car, which was their home and which gave them the freedom to go anywhere they wanted.

At night they parked at a campsite beside Pea Tree Beach where they slept under the stars and swam in the morning, cooking their oatmeal breakfast over a familiar campfire. They all had gotten used to this setup and had even begun to enjoy it. But not Kim; she was adamant that they should live someplace more permanent. Kim was very fond of to-do lists, and the number one thing on her to-do list was *Find a house.* She had done this once before, when she'd led her siblings through dangerous woods and found an abandoned cabin on Wabo Point. The owner of the cabin had turned out to be Kimo's father, Johnny Trout.

Now Kim glanced over at Kimo and saw that he was looking at her too. They were only a few months apart in age and their names were almost the same, so they liked to think they were almost twins and could read each other's minds. Maybe they could, because at that moment Kimo was also thinking about the cabin on Wabo Point and how things had gone so wrong when his father returned. A look of worry clouded Kimo's face.

"Don't," Kim said quickly, then changed the subject. "Why would anyone hide diamonds in a rump roast?"

"I'd hide them in a freezer with some ice cubes," said Kimo, grateful to be thinking about something besides his father. "Or maybe I'd hide them in a bank."

"Smart," said Toby.

Pippa wiped her glasses on her T-shirt and scoffed, "You wouldn't steal them in the first place. You're not a villain."

"But if I were..." said Kimo.

"You wouldn't be," said Pippa, putting back on the glasses that magnified the dark freckles around her eyes. "You're not greedy. Villains are always greedy."

"Villains weren't always villains," said Kimo. "Something happened to them to make them that way."

"Spoken like someone who will never be one," snorted Pippa, just as a bright flash of light pierced the windshield. Kim threw a hand up over her eyes. She could hardly see the road now, but between her fingers the light flashed again. She blinked as if blinking could make the flashing stop, but it couldn't, and for a second she was driving blind. She hit the brakes, steering toward the shoulder, where the little green car rumbled to a stop just as Toby yelled from the backseat, "Look at that!"

Toby was pointing to a creature standing some distance away in the middle of the road. The creature was human in its dimensions but made entirely of metal that glinted in the moonlight.

Kimo shook his head and said, "Are we dreaming?"

"Probably an alien," said Toby, who had always hoped to meet one.

"Alien schmalien," scoffed Pippa. "I don't think an alien would be carrying that." She pointed to the long object that dangled from the creature's hand. It was an ax. Kim, who was a great reader of books, thought the creature looked like the Tin Woodman from Oz, though it seemed to her to be made of a softer kind of metal.

"Whatever it is, it's heading toward us," said Kimo, suddenly nervous. "Roll up your windows! Hurry!" He saw that the metal man was waving its free hand in the air. "What do you think it wants?"

Before any of them could answer, the creature called out, "Help!"

Kim tightened her grip on the steering wheel. What to do? She looked at Kimo and asked, "Should I drive?"

"Please, help!" the creature called out again, and

Kimo thought how it would be irresponsible of him to let a giant metal man carrying an ax get any nearer to his brother and sisters. On the other hand, he and his siblings had had their own share of trouble in life and were sympathetic to anyone (or anything) that called out for help. "Let's keep the windows up and ask what it wants," Kimo said to Kim.

Kim nodded, and rolled her window down a crack, shouting to the creature, "We want to help you, but put down your ax or we'll drive away!" The creature, now only a few yards from the car, did as it was told, setting the ax down on the muddy shoulder of the road and raising its hands in surrender.

"All right," said Kim, "you may approach." She was speaking very formally, as if this might defuse the bizarre situation. The metal man took a few more steps toward the car, but just as it was about to reach them, a loud shriek rose up from the maha trees that bordered the road. The children turned and saw the dark sky full of even darker wings.

Thousands of birds—screaming and cawing—had suddenly flown out of their nests and were circling above.

"What's going on?" This was Toby, who nervously clutched the jar that held his goldfish, Goldie.

"Something scared them," Kim reasoned.

The metal creature was outside the windows now, banging on the glass. "Let me in before it starts!"

"What starts?" Kim shouted back.

"Knockabout!" the metal man shouted just as there came an earth-shattering rumble, the sound of millions of tons of rock being torn apart, the sound of the planet's vast and ancient tectonic plates shifting. The metal man was right; it was a "knockabout," which was what the inhabitants of the island called an earthquake.

The car began to buck like a horse. Its tires were jumping up and down. Then, suddenly, everything around the car was moving, even the road. The maha trees swayed so that first one branch then another bent and touched the ground. It was as if a giant had picked up the earth and was amusing himself with it. Turning it this way and that way. Shaking it. Playing with it like a toy.

Strapped in her car seat, baby Penny began to wail with fear. Pippa, who felt a ferocious and protective love for the baby, scrambled out of her own seat and slid down in front of Penny's so that she could face the baby and hold her hands, comforting her.

Meanwhile the metal creature was outside the bucking car, trying to hold on. It gripped the door handle and shouted, "Let me in!"

Forgetting himself, Kimo reached into the back and flipped up the door lock. The back door swung open, and instantly the metal creature moved into the churning vehicle.

For several long seconds the car bucked up and down, bouncing the children and the metal man around inside it. Then, just as suddenly as it had started, the shaking stopped. Everything went still: the car, the road, the trees. Even the birds stopped their shrieking and quickly disappeared back into their nests in the maha branches.

It took a second for the children to catch their breath and realize the knockabout was over. The danger had passed. It took another second for them to realize that the metal creature was now in the car with them. So the danger hadn't passed. During this second, the creature reached its metal paws up and, with a little tug, began to pull off its metal head.

Toby screamed and covered his eyes, so he didn't see what the others saw: The creature's "head" was really only a big, soft metal mask—like an inside-out oven mitt with eyeholes cut from it. Underneath the mask was the face of a grown-up. She had long black hair and bright green eyes. She was smiling. "You can always tell when something big is coming. The birds fly out of their nests all at once like that. They sense it."

"Sense what?" asked Kimo, who was no longer afraid.

"A knockabout," said Kim, catching the woman's meaning.

"There have been more and more of them lately."

"Yup," the children agreed, almost in unison. They had noticed it too. There were knockabouts every few days when the whole island seemed about to capsize, like a fragile boat tossed on the ocean's surface.

"Thanks for stopping," said the woman, whose enormous eyes made Kimo think of satellite dishes. "My name is Leaf."

"Are you a space alien?" asked Toby, who had uncovered his eyes and was sounding hopeful.

"I'm a scientist," Leaf said, looking around at the patchwork of children. They had varying degrees of brown hair and brown skin. Some had black eyes and some had green.

"Scientist?" Pippa was confused. "What's with

the getup? You look like something from a horror movie."

"I study plants that grow around the crater of the volcano," Leaf answered. "This is a lava suit. I wear it so I can get close to the volcano and take samples of the plants without getting burned."

"There are plants that grow on volcanoes?" Kimo had studied volcanoes in school and didn't remember hearing about that.

"Of course there are," said Leaf, opening her eyes even wider. "You should know about volcanoes. You're an islander."

"He's a Fitzgerald-Trout," said Kim. She didn't like the way the woman never seemed to blink, but just stared at them with those flying-saucer eyes.

"Whoever you are. You should know about the place where you live. You should know that volcanoes destroy most plants completely." Now Leaf's voice dropped to a whisper so the children had to lean close to hear her. "If you don't know that, then you won't be able to help when you're needed."

"*Needed?* Who needs us?" This was Toby, whispering into the air. Kim and Kimo looked at each other, unsettled.

But Leaf didn't answer the question. Instead she said, "Mount Muldoon has started leaking lava. It's a dormant volcano, but it's woken up. Ask the birds—they fly out of their trees whenever the lava comes."

Kim noticed that Leaf's eyes sparkled as she said this; the woman seemed to be excited at the thought of the volcano spewing fiery liquid rock. The thought made Kim shudder. "We'd better get out of here," she said, starting the car.

"Wait," said Leaf, opening the door. "Let me grab my ax." The children looked at one another. They didn't trust grown-ups, especially grown-ups with axes. Pippa, who had a temper that rivaled even the fiercest volcano, growled at

Leaf, "You have to put your ax in the trunk." Her brown freckles darkened as she spoke, making her look like she might explode.

"All right," said Leaf, giving a small shrug and running to get the ax.

"Well done," Kimo said to Pippa, then added, "just like this rump roast."

MOON EAR TATION

CHAPTER
2

The ride to Leaf's research station at the foot of Mount Muldoon was very uncomfortable. Toby had to sit on Pippa's lap in the backseat and she kept accusing him of squashing her. "You're grinding your bones into my legs," she snapped.

"I'm not trying to," Toby groused. He didn't speak very often so it was a measure of his annoyance that he was talking now.

Leaf kept saying how sorry she was and how

much she appreciated the ride. "It's not your fault he has sharp bones," Pippa said.

"It's my fault he has to sit on your lap," Leaf offered.

"I do not have sharp bones," Toby wailed. He looked for a second like he might cry, but then he pulled himself together and glared at Pippa.

"You sure have sharp eyes," Pippa said. It was true. Toby's glare could change the weather in a room.

Kim and Kimo looked at each other out of the corners of their eyes. They were both thinking the same thing: Grown-ups make everything difficult. Take their parents, for example. Between them, the children had five different mothers and fathers; their family tree was impossible to keep track of, but the one thing that was clear was that all five of their parents were terrible. For instance, none of them had offered the children a place to live; instead those five parents had left the children to fend for themselves, living on their own in the little green car that they parked at the beach.

The children's parents were so terrible that the Fitzgerald-Trouts considered themselves lucky not to have to live with any of them.

Kim, Pippa, and Toby would not have wanted to live with their father, Dr. Fitzgerald, a scientist who had moved them all into the car before he'd flown off to a different, distant island to pursue his research. Nor would they have wanted to live with Pippa and Kim's greedy mother, Maya, who had been thrown in jail for stealing billions of dollars.

Kimo, Toby, and Penny's mother was Tina. She was a country-and-western singer whose songs sometimes topped the island's music charts. Tina was a very vain woman who, when she visited the children, spent half her time checking her reflection in a mirror or window. The other half she spent telling the children how terrible *they* looked. She told Kim to brush her hair, Kimo to clean his clothes, Pippa to sit up straight, and Toby to wipe his nose. As for baby Penny, who was less than a year old and had been left in the car by Tina with a bag of diapers and eighty dollars, Tina now claimed that the baby was getting fat. "You need to put that baby on a diet," she snarked at the older children.

"A baby can't go on a diet!" Pippa shouted in a flash of anger. It was bad enough that Tina had abandoned the baby to the care of her siblings, but now she was criticizing the way the older children were raising the baby. Pippa had frowned at her and said, "You don't understand a thing about babies."

Tina had shaken her head and wagged her finger at Pippa. "Don't frown. It makes the skin on your face wrinkle. You don't want worry lines. They're very unattractive." The moment became legendary among the children, who would often turn to one another when times were tough and say, "You don't want worry lines. They're very unattractive."

Penny's father was Tina's husband, a man

named Clive who was often seen around the island wearing a blue tuxedo that matched his blue convertible. Penny—who was bald—looked a lot like Clive, but that was the only way to tell that he was her father. The few times Clive had brought envelopes of money to the children (so that they could buy food and diapers), he was careful not to get close to the baby. "I think I'm allergic," he explained to the older children. "That time I held her, I broke out in hives." A father allergic to his baby? The Fitzgerald-Trouts had always known there were a million ways to be a terrible parent, but now they knew there were a million and one.

As bad as Clive was, he couldn't compete with Kimo's terrible father, Johnny Trout. As far as all of them were concerned, Johnny was the worst parent of all because of what had happened the night he'd returned to his cabin on Wabo Point.

Thinking about this brought Kim back to thinking about her to-do list and the number one thing on that list: *Find a house*. Not having one was making her worry more than usual. She frowned and then immediately heard Tina's nagging voice in her head. But it was Kimo who spoke: "You don't want worry lines. They're very unattractive." He and Kim both laughed. They really had been thinking the same thing.

"We're almost there," Leaf said, causing Kim to startle. For a few minutes, she had forgotten the scientist was in the car. "I really appreciate the ride. I hope it wasn't out of your way."

"We don't have a way," Kim offered. "It's summer and school's out so we're taking a vacation."

"We're driving around the island," Kimo added.

"Seeing beaches we've never seen." That was Pippa.

They could have told the woman that they needed a home and that they were on the lookout for an abandoned house, but the Fitzgerald-Trouts were private children and very proud, with an innate mistrust of grown-ups. There was no way they were going to admit their situation to this one.

"Sounds like fun," Leaf said, and no one disagreed with her. It *was* fun even if they all had to sleep in the car on nights when it rained. "Turn right," Leaf said, pointing to a narrow dirt road that cut a path through the trees. Kim flicked on her turn signal and maneuvered onto the bumpy road. They drove in silence, watching the headlights paint the maha trees.

After a few minutes, they pulled up in front of a small wooden building. The sign out front read MOON EAR TATION.

"What's moon ear tation?" Kim asked.

"Sounds like a disease," said Kimo. "Something that makes you dizzy."

"Do you study the moon?"

"I like the font," Pippa said. "Helvetica." Pippa was crazy about fonts and knew the names of all of them. "But the spacing is all wrong."

"It's supposed to say Muldoon Research Station," Leaf explained, "but the sign is made out of mushimush wood, which the jabberwills have been eating. They crawl out of their burrows at night and chew up the letters."

"I wouldn't live anyplace where there were jabberwills," Kimo said.

"They're perfectly harmless," Leaf said. "They have long teeth, but they only eat plants. Not people."

"Be careful anyway," Kimo warned.

"It is very odd," mused Leaf. "I've never known jabberwills to eat mushimush wood. They don't usually have a taste for it." She shook her head. "The forests are changing."

"How?" Toby asked.

But Leaf didn't answer directly; instead she mused, "Don't you love this island?" She was staring out into the darkness and her eyes were lit up like the car's headlights. Kimo was watching her intently, and it struck him that she was not only mysterious but a little bit spooky. All she needed was a black hat and a cauldron and she would be the perfect Halloween witch. The thought sent shivers up his spine. He wished she would just get out of the car, but she had lowered her voice to a whisper, saying, "If something is important to you, you've got to be willing to make a sacrifice for it...."

Blah, blah, blah, thought Kim, who had stopped listening. She was tapping the steering wheel impatiently. This is what happens when you give a grown-up a ride. They start trying to teach you a lesson.

"Aren't you getting out?" snapped Pippa, who, like Kim, was feeling impatient.

"Yes. Right," said Leaf. "Thanks again." For the first time since she'd gotten in the car, she blinked. Then she smiled, quickly opened the door, and climbed out.

In the rearview mirror, Kim watched her go around to the back of the car to get her ax. Kim pushed the trunk button and the trunk popped open. She heard Leaf reaching into the trunk and then she heard the trunk slam, but as soon as it was down, Leaf was no longer standing there.

"Where'd she go?" Kim asked, turning around and looking out the windows.

"Huh," Kimo said. "One second she was there. The next second she wasn't." They all rolled their windows down and stuck out their heads, gazing around the wide, dark patch of dirt between the car and the research station. There was no sign of Leaf.

"Leaf? Are you there?" the children called out to her. There was no answer except the buzz of the brizzill bugs that were dive-bombing the car's headlights.

"She vanished," Pippa said, rolling up her window to keep the bugs out.

"Pretty spooky for a scientist," said Kimo.

"She was no scientist," said Toby.

"Of course she was." Kim couldn't stand it when Toby made comments that seemed to come out of nowhere. Next he was going to say that the woman was an alien.

"No," said Toby, adamant, "she wasn't. She was—"

"She must have run to the building when we weren't looking," Kim interrupted. She didn't see how this was possible, but it was the only logical explanation.

"When the trunk slammed we got distracted," said Kimo. "Somehow we missed seeing her go."

Toby didn't think this made sense. He was sure he had a better explanation, but he was a boy of very few words and no one was interested in listening to him, so he just whispered under his breath, "The nose knows."

Pippa said with a smirk, "Maybe a jabberwill ate her." Then she let loose a terrifying cackle.

CHAPTER
3

The night that followed their introduction to the plant scientist was a wet and sleepless one for the Fitzgerald-Trouts. Instead of going to Pea Tree Beach, they parked at the base of Mount Muldoon near a picnic site beside a narrow river that ran down from the mountain. As they pulled into the makeshift parking lot drops of rain began to splatter against the windshield, and the children all groaned, knowing that if the rain continued they would have to sleep in the car instead of outside on the grassy riverbank. Fitting all of them into the car had been uncomfortable in the past before they'd found Penny. Now that the backseat had her car seat in it, sleeping in the car was nearly impossible, especially for Pippa and Toby, who had to sit upright in the back without the luxury of seats that reclined.

But the rain didn't care how uncomfortable the Fitzgerald-Trouts were. It was throwing itself down like a toddler having a tantrum, and by the time the children had brushed their teeth (wetting their mouths with rainwater and then spitting the toothpaste froth out their windows), drops of rain as large as mushimush berries were hammering down on the roof. "It sounds like we're inside someone's stomach," Toby said before he could stop himself. He was excited by the idea and the words came tumbling out.

"Or we're inside some*thing*'s stomach," countered Pippa. "What if the whole car got swallowed by a T. rex and now we're making our way through its digestive tract?"

"We'd know if we'd got eaten by a T. rex," said Toby, but his voice wavered because he wasn't sure. He lapsed into silence made more dramatic by the pounding of the rain. After a second he blurted out, "*Would* we know?"

"Yes we would," Kim assured him.

But Pippa trilled, "Don't be too sure! That could be stomach acid pouring down around us right now."

"Stop scaring him," Kim scolded.

"I'm not scared," said Toby, who was definitely scared. Then he noticed that Pippa was giving baby Penny her bottle of milk. Toby knew that if Pippa were really worried she wouldn't be feeding the baby, she would be holding the baby in her arms, protecting her. Toby stuck his tongue out at Pippa. "You made it up."

Pippa shrugged and said, "So what?"

Kim wadded up a sweatshirt to use as a pillow and pressed it against the window. She closed her eyes and began to review the day that had passed and make plans for the next. Tomorrow we will find a house, she thought, without much conviction. I did it before and I'll do it again. *I can, I can, I can,* she said to herself, as if by saying it, she could make herself believe it. Then she thought that perhaps it had been sheer luck that she'd happened upon Johnny Trout's empty cabin. How could something that good possibly happen again? But she wouldn't let the others know she felt such dismay. "Good night," she called out, in what she thought sounded like a hopeful voice.

"Night," they all shouted back, because the rain was becoming so loud they had to shout to be heard. Kimo tilted his seat back as far as it would go and leaned his head against the window. He could tell from the pounding on the roof that the raindrops were getting larger. The word *deluge* floated into his head, and for some reason that word made him think of his father. Until recently, Johnny Trout had been sailing across the ocean and Kimo hadn't known whether his father was alive or not. During that time, Kimo had often imagined his father out on the open sea, and when it rained, he would wonder if his father was being rained on too. Kimo pined for his father and would sometimes entertain himself by imagining their reunion. Someday they would meet again and it would be great.

Don't think about him, Kimo told himself now, but the sound of the rain on the car's roof brought back the memory so strongly that Kimo couldn't fight it.

He was in the kitchen of Johnny Trout's cabin baking a ginker cake for a school party. The cabin door had opened and Johnny Trout had walked in. He looked like a pirate: his dirty, matted hair covered with a filthy bandanna; his face bearded and scarred. He wore no shirt and his torn pants—which looked like they had been made from old canvas sailcloth—were stiff with dried seawater. Long, twisted toenails emerged from his bare, bruised feet. Looking down at those feet, Kimo saw that Johnny Trout was followed close on his heels by a large pig. Wendell, Kimo thought, having heard that his father had taken a pig with him on his sailing voyage.

As if the pig had heard his name called, he had sniffed the air in Kimo's direction. "Hrrk-hrrk-hrrk," he grunted suddenly, and charged toward the boy, who was holding baby Penny across his chest in a sling. Wendell's mouth was open, baring large, gleaming, sharp teeth. "Hrrk-hrrk-hrrk!" Whether the pig was going for Penny or for Kimo wasn't clear. What was clear was that the pig would tear flesh from whomever it got to first.

"Move!" Johnny yelled. Kimo didn't need to be told twice. He was already running toward the door, flinging it open and racing into the tall grass that grew around the cabin. He stood there, outside the cabin, catching his breath in the moonlight as the other children stumbled out one by one.

They waited, hearts racing, wiping nervous sweat from their foreheads. "What a horrible pig," Kim gasped.

"Someone should make him into sausage," Pippa snarled, trying to break the tension. "They should fry that pig up and serve him to the *Ham!* contestants." *Ham!* was a popular TV show on the island in which contestants shoved sausages into their mouths while telling jokes. This idea made Toby laugh, and Kimo pretended to chuckle. He could tell his siblings were doing their best to cheer him up.

"What do we do now?" Pippa asked. No one knew and so they just stood there in the tall grass, waiting. Was Johnny locking the pig up in a room or maybe putting him on a leash so that he couldn't hurt anyone? They heard a door slam and then the sound of Johnny whistling somewhere in the cabin.

A second later the old pirate stepped outside. "Sorry about that." Johnny pulled the door shut behind him. "Wendell's protective. We've been traveling together a long time. There were nights I was anchored on islands that didn't even have names, islands that weren't on the map. I didn't know what animals might be waiting, hungry, in the dark. I trained him to be on guard. I also trained him to fetch. You should see him."

The children didn't say a word. None of them was very impressed by Johnny's description of the pig. It seemed to them that most pets could fetch something or other. They all lapsed into silence, until Kimo finally got up his nerve and said, "Hi, Dad."

"Hey, kid," Johnny replied. "Long time no see." It was an understatement. By Kimo's calculation he hadn't seen his father in at least seven years. Wasn't that enough time for every single cell in his body to have been replaced at least once? He thought he remembered that from science class. But he didn't bring it up. Instead he smiled at his father and said, "I'd like to hear about those islands. The ones without names, I mean. In fact, I'd like to hear about your whole trip.... What happened? What adventures did you have?"

Johnny crossed his arms over his chest and put his hands into his armpits, like he was trying to keep them warm, then he sighed and said, "A lot of adventures. Some you wouldn't believe. You know what? Someday I'll write them down. You can read the book. Tonight, I'm tired. Can't remember the last time I slept. It's been days, weeks maybe. I'd better get to bed." He turned and opened the door. "See ya," he said, heading into the cabin.

"Wait." Kimo stopped him. "You're going?"

"To bed, yeah." Johnny blinked. "Didn't I just say that?"

"But what about us?" Kimo was genuinely confused. Was his long-lost father really leaving them outside his cabin in the dark?

"Huh." Johnny adjusted his bandanna more

squarely on his head. "You've got a car. You'll find someplace else." With that, Johnny slipped inside and the door creaked shut behind him. Then they heard the unmistakable sound of the bolt sliding into the lock. He had completely shut them out.

So that was it. That was Kimo's great reunion with his great father. Or, as Pippa described it later, Kimo's awful reunion with his awful father. "In the history of terrible fathers he is one for the ages."

It was so awful that Kimo couldn't even remember what had happened next. Kim—or someone—must have knocked on the door and explained to Johnny that they needed their things. Someone must have gone back into the house to get them because he knew that someone had brought the goldfish's jar to the car and someone else had carried their clothes and he was pretty sure that the binoculars that Pippa now wore around her neck had once belonged to Johnny. And hadn't they taken the ginker cake to school the next day?

Which meant that someone must have gone back into the house to get the cake from the oven.

But it wasn't Kimo. He hadn't gone back in. He'd gone straight to the front passenger seat of the little green car, feeling like he wanted to cry. But he hadn't cried. Why hadn't he? Maybe to cry he would have had to believe it. But he didn't believe it. He was still in shock.

Now, with his head against the glass, listening to the sky pouring its water over them, Kimo once again wished that he could cry. It had been at least a month since the night of the reunion and he still hadn't shed a single tear. What was wrong with him?

Then he thought, What if the rain on the roof is really the sound of my own crying? What if I finally let all the tears flood out? Before he could think another thought, the tears were there, brimming over his eyes and washing down his cheeks. Kimo cried and cried as the rain roared louder, a deluge so noisy they might have been in a car wash.

An unfathomable volume of rain fell that night. Kimo would find out just how much when he woke the next morning to a loud shout of horror from Toby, followed by Pippa's scream, "Shut the door!" Kimo jerked out of his half sleep and turned around in his seat in time to catch a glimpse of Toby yanking shut the door as water poured onto the floor. Just then Kimo felt the water around his own ankles, and he pulled his feet up onto his seat. "What happened?"

"The river..." said Kim, who had also just woken and snatched her own wet feet up. Kim didn't need to say any more because by then Kimo was looking out the window and could see that the little green car was completely surrounded by dirty brown water—for as far as the eye could see!

It was as if the car were sitting in the middle of a lake.

There was no sign of the river itself except for a line of trees that must have once stood on its bank but now rose up directly out of the water.

"There was so much rain that the river overflowed," said Kim.

"It's a flood," said Kimo, and for a second the thought flashed through his mind that his tears from the night before had caused it, but the thought was quickly replaced by Kimo's certainty that the crying couldn't have caused something bad since it had made him feel so much better.

"I can't believe you opened the door," Pippa snarled at Toby. She was grumpy from her bad night's sleep.

"How should I know?"

"You could've used your eyes," she groused. "There's water everywhere." Toby bonked her on the head, and she grabbed his hair.

"Stop fighting," Kim said with authority. "You're

going to teach the baby bad habits." This quieted Pippa and Toby, who knew that she was right.

Kimo grew practical. "The water's moving. Is the car?"

"I don't think so," Kim answered. She was staring out the windows, watching the water that seemed to be flowing away from the mountain and in the direction of the far-off ocean. Kim studied the trees for some hint that the car was moving in relation to them, but the car seemed to be staying in the same place.

"You think the car will work?" Kimo asked.

"Maybe," Kim said. "Depends on how deep it is."

"It goes past the doors of the car," said Toby, who knew that from having opened one of them.

"If it's over the engine, the car won't start," Kim said, reaching for the key.

"Wait," Kimo said, "there's water everywhere. Once you start driving you're going to have to drive until we find dry land. And what if the water gets deeper? What if the engine does get flooded?"

"What are you saying?" Kim snapped. "We can't just sit here."

"He's saying," said Pippa, "we should eat before we do anything else."

Almost as if she understood, baby Penny— who had also woken when Toby shouted—began to cry, a big ragged yowl of hunger.

"It's okay with me," Kim said as Pippa plugged a pacifier into the baby's mouth. "It's not raining anymore so there's not going to be more water."

"What food do we have that's not in the trunk?"

Toby, who was always hungry and kept snacks close at hand, dipped into a grocery bag that sat at his feet. It was soaked with water, but he rifled around and found three cans of sausages and a plastic tube of crackers: a perfect breakfast as far as the Fitzgerald-Trouts were concerned.

"I don't know about the rest of you," said Kimo, "but I need to stretch." He was already rolling down his window and sliding out of his seat.

He hoisted himself through the window and disappeared. They could hear him sitting down on the roof above them. The others looked at one another and wordlessly followed Kimo's lead, each of them sliding out of their own window and climbing onto the roof. Pippa went last and only after she'd held Penny (and her doll, Lani) out the window, over the dirty brown water, so that Kimo could grab the baby and lift her up onto the roof too.

Penny gurgled with delight and a trickle of drool slid out the corner of her mouth as she and her doll settled down onto Kimo's lap and looked out at the watery world.

It was a small space for the five of them, but they did their best to contain their knees and elbows as they snapped open the cans of sausages and piled them onto the crackers, eating their breakfast feast. A picnic on the roof! This was unlike anything the Fitzgerald-Trouts had ever done before. Pippa and Toby, who often argued, were sharing a rare moment of mutual thrill and excitement. Both were enjoying the salty, delicious tang of the sausages and the crackers. Both were delighted by the water, which made everything around them seem magical. A family of puk-puk geese came into view, floating—somehow in unison—toward the little car. As the geese got closer, the children saw that they were all seated on an upside-down lawn chair that was half submerged in the water and making its way downstream.

"Cool," Toby said.

"Indeed," Pippa echoed. (*Indeed* was a word that all the kids in Pippa's grade had started saying, and Pippa was no exception.)

Kimo and Kim did not share the younger Fitzgerald-Trouts' feelings of delight. "Something

strange is happening on this island," Kimo said, shaking his head. "Has there ever been a flood like this before?"

"There are always floods during the rainy season," said Kim. She raised her eyebrows and pressed her lips together, signaling to Kimo that they shouldn't be talking about things that might worry the others. Kimo nodded at Kim, indicating that he understood and wouldn't keep talking, but he and Kim followed the invisible thread of the same thought.

They thought about this rainy season, much longer and with many more floods than either of them had ever seen before. They thought about the knockabouts that were more and more frequent these days. They thought about what the scientist had told them about the dormant volcano that was waking up. Floods, knockabouts, volcanoes…Something very strange was happening to their island. It's like the time Pippa got sick, Kimo thought, and he knew Kim was thinking it too. *Remember how Pippa had a fever and sweats and then she threw up? That's what the island is doing. The island is sick.*

"I wonder..." Kimo said out loud.

"Shh," Kim said. She didn't want to talk about it. She had too much to worry about already, and too much to do. She thought about her to-do list. She hadn't been able to write the list down since she'd lost her little notebook. In fact, one of the items on her to-do list was to buy a new notebook where she could write down her to-do lists. But she was so busy with so many other things that she hadn't managed to do even that yet. She was absolutely fixated on the number one item on her (mental) list. *Find a house. I can, I can, I can,* she repeated to herself, then she turned to Pippa and poked her in the ribs. "Hand me the binoculars."

Pippa leaned over the edge of the car and reached back in through the window, grabbing the binoculars that hung from a hook. She handed them to Kim. "What do you want them for?"

"I need to see where the water ends," Kim said,

raising them to her eyes and surveying their sur-
roundings. It was a gray day. The sky seemed to be
made entirely of gray wool, and the trees and water
were cloaked in it too. In every direction all she could
see was woolly sky and watery land stitched together
by the occasional line of treetops. She lowered the
binoculars. "There's nothing but water anywhere."

Pippa, who was a wonderful artist, was wishing
she had a sketchbook or at the very least some loose
paper so that she could sketch what she was seeing.
Not having any way to doodle made her grumpy.
"What are we gonna do?" she groaned. "We can't
just sit on the roof and wait for the water to go away."

"We have to try to get out of here," said Kimo.
"I think we should follow the trees that grow in a
line along the road."

"Let's try to find a dry place where we can stay
till the water retreats," said Kim.

"If it retreats," said Pippa.

"It probably will," said Kimo. "It's stopped
raining, and all the water is heading for the ocean."

It was true; the water was flowing down from the mountain and away to the sea.

No one said anything for a while. They watched as a large broken branch with a beehive still attached floated past them. The bees buzzed around it, seemingly baffled by their new, wet circumstances.

After a moment, Kimo shrugged and said, "Ready?"

"We've gotta make sure we don't drive into deep water." Kim grimaced.

"Don't frown." Pippa raised an eyebrow. "You don't want worry lines. They're very unattractive." They all laughed, and Kim thought about Tina. No matter how bad things got, at least they didn't have to live with her; at least they were banded together on the roof of the car and not being bossed around by some terrible grown-up.

As if agreeing with Kim, the sun decided at that moment to break through the woolly sky. It cast a warm beam of light over the Fitzgerald-Trouts.

"Hey," said Pippa, suddenly struck by an idea, "I think I know how we can get out of here."

CHAPTER
4

Pippa's idea was this: She and Kimo—who were tall enough that the water wouldn't reach over their waists—would walk in front of the car with long sticks. They would lower the sticks into the water until the sticks touched the road. That way they could make sure the water wasn't so deep that it would reach the car's engine. They would lead the car onto the road and then against the currents toward higher ground.

Kimo thought they might not be able to walk

fast enough to stay ahead of the car, but Kim liked Pippa's plan and assured him that she would drive very slowly. Toby, who wasn't tall enough to help, offered to sit on top of the roof with the binoculars, watching out for landmarks. Kim couldn't imagine what he might see that would be in any way helpful, but since one of the things on her to-do list was *Be nicer to Toby*, she decided not to point this out to him.

Excited by the adventure, Kimo and Pippa slid off the roof and set out through the water toward some far-off bushes—the tops of which were just sticking out of the water—to search for sticks. Kim slipped through the window and into the car, then took Penny from Toby and changed her diaper before fastening the baby into her car seat.

When they were all ready, Kim started the engine and slowly pressed on the gas. For a second, the tires spun in the mud, but then they found purchase and the car jolted forward through the murky water that splashed up on either side.

Slowly, slowly the little green car forged through the floodwaters. Pippa and Kimo were walking ten yards or so in front, stopping every few steps to measure the depth of water. They were leading Kim away from the picnic area and toward the path between the trees that marked the actual road. She watched them walking and carefully measuring and noticed that between measurements they would sometimes wheel their hands around in the air and then slap themselves on the face or neck. Just as she was wondering what exactly was going on, Toby slid in through the window. Apparently he had given up his post on the roof.

"Brizzill bugs," he said. So that explained the slapping. Kimo and Pippa must have been chasing away the bugs, trying not to get bitten.

"It's the rain," Kim explained. "The more rain, the more bugs."

"I got a billion bites," said Toby.

Outside the car, Kimo and Pippa were slapping brizzill bugs and measuring the water depth with their sticks while carrying on a conversation about their encounter with Leaf, the scientist. "Do you think she really goes on the edges of volcanoes or was that a story?" *Slap, slap.*

"Why else would she have the metal suit?" *Slap.*

"Metal conducts heat," said Pippa. "It doesn't make sense to wear something that conducts heat when you're going near something hot, like a volcano." *Slap, slap.*

"But metal doesn't burn—so that part makes sense."

"None of it makes sense," said Pippa. "I mean, what was she doing up on the mountain all alone anyway?"

It was a good question, and if Toby had been there he might have given them the answer. He might have said the thing he had wanted to say the night before when Kim had interrupted him. But

Toby wasn't there, and Kimo had no such explanation. Instead he dipped his stick into the water and felt something hard underneath it. "The road!"

Things moved a little faster once the car was on the asphalt. Kim was still driving through water, of course, but the asphalt was more even and after a while Kimo and Pippa realized they weren't even measuring anymore because the road was always at the same depth. They kept walking in front of the car anyway, like they were leading a parade.

"I wonder how far the water goes," Pippa mused. "Maybe we should find a road that goes up—" But Pippa didn't get a chance to finish her thought because Kim was shouting at them from the car, "Look!"

Of all the crazy things they'd seen floating by that morning, this was the craziest of all. It was a large metal bathtub with a tall shower pole attached to it. Instead of being full of water like a bathtub should be, the tub was empty. But it was surrounded by floodwater, which they now all noticed held a reflection of the clouds overhead. A lava gull sat on the edge of the tub, peering down at the clouds in the murky water. The bird looked confused by the whole arrangement.

"He's lost," said Pippa, who knew something about the habits of lava gulls. "Too far inland. He couldn't tell where the ocean ended and the land started."

"I'm not talking about the gull," shouted Kim, who had stopped the car in the middle of the flooded road. Kimo and Pippa walked over to her window.

"The tub is floating down a driveway." Kim pointed to the stretch of water between two rows of bushes, and they saw that the tub was indeed coming down what must have been a long driveway. Behind the bathtub was a trail of other floating furniture—a bookshelf, a coffee table, a trash can, a rocking chair. They couldn't see what was at the end of the trail of furniture, but now they understood what Kim meant. If there was furniture floating down a flooded driveway, that meant at the end of the driveway there was a flooded house.

"A flooded house is an abandoned house," Kim said. "Let's go take a look."

Kim drove the car off the road and up onto a high embankment, then they unloaded the baby and the goldfish from the car. The water on the road had been only over their knees, but they didn't know how deep the water in the driveway was going to be so they decided they had to be prepared to swim. Kim took the large plastic cooler out of the trunk and they quickly consumed its contents— a half-full carton of milk, four tubes of yogurt, and a package of salami—then they tossed the last of the cooler's ice onto the muddy embankment. Once the cooler was empty, Kim settled the baby (and her doll) and the goldfish (in his jar) into it, leaving the lid open. She tucked a few extra diapers and a blanket next to the baby. Now the cooler and its cargo would float like a raft, so the baby and Goldie could be carried safely alongside them on their trip.

They started down from the car to the wet road and then turned in the direction of the driveway, which must have sloped downhill because the children immediately felt the water rise around them. "This is a bad idea," said Toby, who was the shortest. "How deep is it going to get?"

"The more water there is, the more likely we are to find a house that no one wants," Kim answered. None of the others could argue with that.

Silently they moved farther down the driveway, deeper into the water.

Toby was the first to start swimming. He flipped over onto his back and pointed his head down the driveway, kicking backward toward his goal. A few minutes later, Pippa began to do frog kicks with her head out of the water. Soon they were all swimming.

Kimo, who was the strongest swimmer, kept the cooler floating in the water in front of him. With each stroke, he pushed it a little bit ahead, playfully flicking water at Penny. The baby cooed, seemingly amused by the wobbly raft trip. The goldfish, who should have been happy at the sight of all that water, looked more uncertain.

They swam the length of several swimming pools until they rounded a bend in the treetops. Suddenly, in front of them, loomed a rickety, wooden two-story house, flooded almost to the top of its first-floor windows. As they approached the house, Kim quickened her stroke, heading toward the wooden beam above the doorway.

"Here I go," she said, taking a deep gulp of air and diving down.

Underwater, she propelled herself through the open front door and swam for the surface.

A moment later, she was banging on a window,
shouting out to the others, "All clear!"

CHAPTER
5

Is anyone home?" The children were treading water in the middle of what had once been the living room and shouting toward the upstairs. "Anyone home?" Their voices echoed, bouncing between the water and the walls, so they heard the word *home* repeated over and over. There was no reply.

"I hope it's okay that we're here." It had only just occurred to Kim that they might be trespassing.

"We're castaways," reasoned Kimo. "There's practically a whole ocean of water outside, so there's nothing wrong with climbing aboard a passing ship. Those are the rules of the sea."

"True," said Kim. "And as long as the house is flooded like this, they won't come back." They all agreed with this logic.

Now that they were inside, the place felt smaller. The water was so high that a chandelier, which hung from the ceiling, was touching the top of it. Toby and Pippa, tired from the long swim, hung on to the chandelier's chain, surveying the room, which was full of floating objects: small pieces of furniture but also shoes, umbrellas, books, baskets, teacups, a globe. Anything light enough to float that had been unmoored at the time of the flood was now drifting on the surface of the water. Still holding Goldie, Toby picked up the globe and tossed it like a ball to Kimo. Kimo tossed it to Pippa, who tossed it to Kim. They played a spirited game of keep-away until Penny began to wail in that mysterious way babies do when they want something but can't tell you what it is. "I think she needs a nap," Kimo said, tossing the globe up into the air like a seal.

"She napped in the car," said Kim, who had found footing on the dining room table, which was made from something so heavy that it still rested at the bottom of the flooded room.

"She's probably hungry," said Pippa. Kim realized with a groan that they had left the bag of food in the car.

"I'll find the kitchen," said Kimo, swimming toward the back of the house. "You guys go upstairs." After a few strokes, he reached the end of the hall and swam through the open doorway into the kitchen. He made straight for an upper cupboard that was out of the water, and he saw that the top shelves held dozens of boxes of something called "digestive biscuits." Whoever lived in the house must have had stomach trouble and stockpiled the comforting food. Kimo crammed as many boxes as he could into a wooden salad bowl and swam back down the hallway, then up the stairs. He found his siblings sprawled on a thick carpet on the house's second floor, trying to comfort the baby, who was still wailing.

"Here," Kimo said, tearing open a box of biscuits. Penny took the treat with greedy fingers and her crying instantly stopped. Breathing a collective sigh of relief, the others fell into a happy silence. There is nothing like a crying baby to make you appreciate the quiet.

It had been a long morning full of wet excitement, and now they were enjoying the thick carpet (warmed by a beam of sunshine that came pouring through the high windows) and the digestive biscuits, which turned out to be very sweet and more like cookies. "We did it," said Kim. "We found a house." The words in her head—*I can, I can, I can*—had changed to *I did, I did, I did*. She had her eyes closed and was, for the first time in many weeks, feeling utterly, happily relaxed. As long as the house was flooded, she felt certain that no one would want it but them.

"I think I love digestive biscuits," said Kimo.

"'Comfort for the humble stomach,'" said Pippa, reading the package, then she added, "What does that even mean?"

Toby crumbled a few biscuits into Goldie's jar, then he tapped it. This was his signal to the fish that it was time to eat. Goldie rose to the surface and began to gulp down the crumbs. So his humble stomach was being comforted too.

"Come on," said Pippa, getting to her feet, "let's explore."

Kimo nodded and got up, realizing how wonderful it was to stand on two legs again. He bent down to pick up Penny and saw that the baby had curled herself around her doll, stuck her thumb in her mouth, and fallen asleep. "Shh." He put his fingers to his lips. The others nodded in agreement. With Penny napping, they would each have the freedom to do exactly what they wanted for a few quiet hours.

Kim wandered into one of the bedrooms that had high bookshelves. She was looking for a book that she could curl up with for an afternoon of reading, but before she had even crossed the room to the shelf, her eyes landed on an open closet. In the closet she was shocked to see several long shelves that held nothing but shoes: hundreds and hundreds of pairs of shoes. I haven't yet explained to you that none of the children on the island ever wore shoes. Only the adults wore shoes. So Kim was completely unfamiliar with the variety of shoes that a grown-up can have. Now curiosity got the best of her, and she began to inspect them.

There were red sneakers for running and white sneakers for playing tennis; high sneakers for basketball and low sneakers for no reason she knew of. There were flip-flops in three or four different colors. There were river sandals that strapped around your foot so you could safely walk in the water. There were pink ballet slippers and fuzzy bedroom slippers, leather sandals covered in little red and blue beads, and a pair of green slippers with toes! There were hiking boots, cowboy boots, rain boots, horseback riding boots, and ski boots. There were boots for work, made of leather dyed brown and black and red and yellow. Some went up past the knee, some stopped at the ankle. As many boots as there were, there were even more high heels. High heels of every imaginable color, pattern, and height. Kim lifted a pair off the shelf and slipped them on. They were shiny and black. She stood up, wobbling, and took a cautious step; a noise like a little click came from the bottom of the shoe. She took another step and it happened again. She lifted her left foot and looked at the sole of the shoe; a small metal plate was screwed into the toe and another was screwed into the heel. Tap shoes, Kim realized with delight.

She had once seen a movie at the drive-in where a redheaded girl had danced in tap shoes. Watching her, Kim had wondered if she could do it. Now she walked over to the mirror and gave it a try. She did the dance moves just as she remembered them, skipping and clicking and slapping her toes then her heels, heels then her toes: *tap, tap, tap, tap, tip-pity, tap, tap.* It was fantastic—and exhausting, but mostly fantastic. Kim caught her reflection in the mirror and saw that she was grinning from ear to ear. I hope I never grow up and have to wear shoes, she thought, but if I do, I will only ever wear tap shoes. She waved her hands and kicked up her heels. Everywhere I go I will *tap, tap, tap, tap, tap, tap....*

While Kim was tapping in front of the mirror, Kimo and Pippa were exploring a room down the hall that was filled with many wacky contraptions. There was a machine with a little seat that slid back and forth when you pulled on a rope with a handle. "It's like a rowboat." Kimo laughed, looking out the windows at the water that surrounded the house. "We could use a real one of those."

Pippa lay on her stomach on a yoga mat. She

had found some paper and a box of colored pencils and was in her element, lying there sketching the gears and wires of the strange machines. While she drew, Kimo hopped onto a bicycle, pedaling it furiously, but because it was fastened in place with the wheels lifted off the floor, he didn't move forward. "Let me get this straight," he said between gulps of air. "Some grown-up built a bike that goes inside his house so he can stare out the windows and pretend to be outside his house?"

"Sure," said Pippa. She was only half listening.

"I've heard about these things," Kimo said knowingly. "This is how grown-ups exercise. On a bike in the house, instead of outside where they could go somewhere."

"Crazy," said Pippa, adjusting her glasses to better focus on her drawing.

Kimo found a set of moving stairs that went around and around in a circle. The point was to stay on top of them and to climb the set of rotating stairs over and over. Kimo, who was very responsible with money, couldn't believe someone would buy a mechanical set of stairs to put in a house with a staircase. He shook his head. "Would someone please explain to me what is wrong with grown-ups?"

"I'm writing a list right now," snorted Pippa, "if you've got a couple of hundred hours to listen to it." Just then a loud bang came from the room next door. It sounded like something heavy had fallen. They jumped up and rushed into the other room, where they found Toby lying sprawled on a bed on top of an enormous mound of blankets. "You okay?" Pippa was kneeling over Toby, checking his pulse.

"Yeaaaah," the boy said, letting out a wild giggle and pointing to a trapdoor in the ceiling above him.

"Hey," said Pippa, poking him in the ribs. "You did this on purpose."

Kim appeared in the room, holding Penny, who had woken at the sound of the banging. "What happened?"

"He jumped," said Pippa, pointing to the opening in the ceiling.

It turned out Toby had climbed onto one of the bedposts and hoisted himself through the trapdoor in hopes of finding treasure hidden in the house's attic. He had picked around in the dark, not finding much of anything, until he had stumbled on an old wooden chest that he was certain held treasure. When he lifted the lid, he wasn't disappointed. The chest was filled with blankets, and it instantly occurred to the boy that he could toss the blankets down from the attic onto the bed and make a very soft landing pad. Which was exactly what he did.

Before he was even done explaining, the other Fitzgerald-Trouts were climbing up the posts of the bed and hauling themselves into the attic to give it a try.

"Awesome," Pippa said as she launched herself from the hole in the ceiling and fell through the air, landing on the soft blankets and the bed.

"*Wheee!*" Kim shouted.

"Skydiving!" exclaimed Kimo.

Even baby Penny had a try, dropping out of Kim's outstretched arms and through the hole until she landed with a squeal of pleasure on the soft pile.

When they had each tried a dozen times, they decided on a new game. Using pieces of furniture and chairs from around the room, they tied the corners of the blankets a few feet above the ground and built a blanket fort. Once it was constructed and covered all of the room, they crawled into it and lay down next to one another, snuggled in their shelter. Kim thought how funny it was that although they hated being cramped in the little green car, here they were in a big house with lots of room and they were building a small fort to crawl into together. She supposed the difference was that in the fort they all had room to stretch out.

"My humble stomach needs comfort," said Kimo.

"Mine too," said Pippa. So Kim crawled back out and retrieved another box of the biscuits from the salad bowl. Back in the warmth of their blanket nest, she passed the box around.

"A house inside a house," said Pippa dreamily. The thought of this protection made her feel brave. "Who knows a scary story?"

"Manu Diggens told me about these kids last summer at Camp Smithers." It might have been the longest sentence Toby had spoken in weeks, so the others let him keep going without interruption. "Manu and the kids were in their tent when they saw this shadow outside it. It was a man, but instead of fingers he had these long blades—"

The older three couldn't help but interrupt with groans of disappointment.

"Don't tell me, the man swung the blades and the tent was torn to shreds and there was blood everywhere," said Kimo. "That story has been going around forever."

"You wrecked it!" Toby swatted at Kimo's arm.

"It's just a story," said Kim. "This island is full of crazy stories. Shark gods who rescue surfers; mountain goddesses who wander the roads at night; ghosts of old priests; haunted canoes and ancient graves dug by the first settlers. If you listened to them all, you'd never be able to take a step without thinking you were going to burst into flames or fall into a volcano."

"Some of them are true," said Pippa. "Have you guys ever heard of the midnight walkers?"

"That's another one," said Kim. "Totally made up, and if you keep telling these stories, you'll scare Penny."

"Maybe," said Pippa, then she asked a question she'd been wanting to have answered for a long time. "Do you think Penny understands what we say?"

"Not everything," said Kimo. "But some things. She knows words."

"She doesn't talk," said Toby. He was thinking how it was easier to communicate with his goldfish than it was with his little sister.

"It's normal that she doesn't talk," said Pippa. But she was thinking it was not normal at all. Shouldn't a baby who was almost able to crawl be able to say a few things? She turned to the baby, who was rolling on the floor with both feet in her hands. "Can you say 'sister'? Try it. Say 'sister.' 'Sister.' Come on, 'sister'?"

Penny looked at Pippa and opened her mouth. "Baa," she said, releasing a spiral of drool.

"Sister," said Kim, joining in on the game. "Try to say 'sister'?"

"Baa," said Penny, "baa, baa, baa."

"How about ninja?" asked Kimo. "Can you say 'ninja'?" Penny put her foot into her mouth, then laughed as she tickled the roof of her own mouth with her toes.

"Fish," Toby offered. "Try saying 'fish.'"

But the baby could say only "baa, baa, baa."

"It's fine," said Kim. "Toby took a long time to talk. Remember, Kimo?"

"Yup," said Kimo. "I think he was like a year old."

"Toby still hardly talks," said Pippa, then she turned to him. "Say 'sister.' Can you say 'sister'?"

Toby glared at Pippa, then said, "I'm rubber and you're glue. Words bounce off me and stick to you."

"Not bad," Pippa said, feeling strangely impressed with Toby for defending himself against her teasing.

When it was time to eat dinner, Kimo and Kim offered to swim to the kitchen for more food. But as they approached the staircase Kimo noticed that fewer of the steps were wet. "The water's retreated," he said gravely. They both knew that if the water vanished, the house's owners would come back.

"We don't want to give it up yet," Kim said. "We don't know when they're coming back."

"I'm not sticking around to meet them," Kimo said. "No way...." He didn't have to explain to her why he was skittish about a run-in with the house's owners. The scene at the cabin on the night of Johnny Trout's return had been humiliating for all of the Fitzgerald-Trouts, but for Kimo it had also been heartbreaking. He sighed and shook his head. "If the water's gone when we wake up tomorrow, then we have to leave." He crossed his arms over his chest to make his point firmly.

"You're right," said Kim, trying not to let her voice betray her disappointment.

Kimo relaxed a little. "Don't worry," he said. "We'll find another place." But they both knew it wasn't as easy as he made it sound.

Despite the news that the water was retreating, they all enjoyed their dinner. With the water lower, Kim and Kimo had been able to open a kitchen cupboard that wouldn't open before. In it, they'd found two cans of breadsticks, a jar of olives, and a package of bacon bits. It made for a surprisingly delicious meal.

After they ate, they lay in the blanket fort reading the books that Kim had found. Toby didn't know how to read yet, but that didn't matter because what he wanted to do was think. He lay on his side with the goldfish jar on the floor in front of him. He had been thinking a lot lately about how cramped Goldie's life was in his little jar, and how difficult it must be for the goldfish to be jostled around on bumpy roads all the time. He thought about the globe they had played with downstairs, and he began to imagine a place on the globe called Tobyworld, a country that was ruled by a boy and his pet goldfish. There were no towns or roads in Tobyworld; there were only forests, and the forests were full of trees that grew marshmallows. "In Tobyworld," he whispered to the goldfish, "goldfishes don't live in jars, they live in tanks the size of swimming pools. And children don't have to learn to spell or count. Everyone eats marshmallows all the time and no one has to brush their teeth."

"You're right. We should brush our teeth."

This was Kim, who had heard only the last couple of words.

"That's not what I said." Toby was indignant.

"We should anyway," Kim countered. "Brush our teeth. It's getting dark." She was already digging through the cooler, looking at the things they'd brought. After a minute she gave up the search. "I think we left our toothbrushes in the car."

Toby smiled to himself, thinking that perhaps the rules of Tobyworld were beginning to take effect. "We'll brush in the morning," said Kimo.

"Sure we will," said Pippa.

Not in the morning, and maybe not ever, the king of Tobyworld was thinking.

"I'm going to sleep," said Kim, tucking Penny into the cooler. "Night."

"Night," they all chorused, snuggling close to one another as they fell into separate dreams.

The next morning they folded the blankets, closed the trapdoor to the attic, put away the food they hadn't eaten, and wrote a note thanking the house's owner for helping "a few tired and wet castaways."

When they descended the staircase, they found that the water had receded so much they didn't need to swim. They waded through the living room and out the front door, and by the time they had walked up the driveway and reached the road, the water was barely around their ankles.

They climbed the embankment and stood around the little green car in silence, foraging for breakfast from the soggy bag of groceries. "On our way back to the beach, we should stop at the laundromat," Kimo suggested between bites of beef jerky. "We could wash our wet clothes and see if Mr. Knuckles has any new tattoos." Mr. Knuckles was the proprietor of the laundromat who had always been kind to the children. He let them sit at the laundromat for as long as they wanted, eating chocolate bars from the broken vending machine and watching TV.

"What road should we take?" Kim grabbed the binoculars from inside the car and began surveying the landscape. It was true the water had receded, but she wanted to know exactly where it ended.

"Let's go over the mountain," said Kimo. "Higher is dryer."

"Hey," Kim suddenly called out, "look at that!" She was pointing at a large circular shape in the distance beyond some trees.

Pippa snatched away the binoculars and raised them to her eyes. "It's a Ferris wheel. There's some kind of fair. I can see the tents and stuff."

Now it was Toby's turn with the binoculars. He stared through them for a long moment, then lowered them and said solemnly, "We have to ride on that Ferris wheel."

Kim bit her lip and said, "It'll cost money."

"We have enough," said Toby, who had no idea if this was actually true.

"Let me check," said Kimo, poking his head back into the car and opening the glove compartment. He pulled out the envelope where they kept the cash that Tina and Clive gave them. He shuffled through the bills and the coins, then looked up and said, "Forty-two dollars and thirty-six cents."

"Is that enough?" Pippa frowned.

"Well, it should last for three weeks and we're

due for another envelope of money in two. So as long as nothing goes wrong with the car…"

"If something does…?" Kim asked. They had had tire trouble in the past, and the gurgling noise in the engine was worrisome.

"It'll cost a lot more than forty dollars," Kimo said.

"But it's only a Ferris wheel," Toby said in a wheedling voice. "How much can it cost?" Kimo said he thought it would cost the same amount as buying food for a day or two, and Toby swore that he would eat only fruit they picked from trees and *that* didn't cost anything at all.

"Yeah, right," said Pippa. "You say that and then as soon as we get to the fair you'll be begging for a hot dog."

"Will not," cried Toby.

Kim silently agreed with Pippa and thought how irritating Toby's voice could be, but again she reminded herself that one of the things on her (mental) to-do list was *Be nicer to Toby*. Thinking this reminded her of the number one thing on her list—*Find a house*. Suddenly she saw how these two things could be combined.

"We can't afford *not* to go on the Ferris wheel," Kim said.

"That makes no sense," said Pippa.

"While we're up there we can look around from way up high and see if we see an abandoned house. If we *don't* go up on the Ferris wheel, we'll have to drive around looking for a house. That will take a lot of gas and cost a lot of dollars." Even as she was saying it she knew her argument was a little silly. The others must have known it too. But there was the slim possibility that Kim was right—they could see a house from up there—and there was the larger truth that they were all looking for an excuse to do something fun.

"Yes!" Toby shouted, sensing that fun had won.

They quickly climbed back into the car, and Kim drove it down off the embankment and onto the wet road. Pippa and Kimo no longer had to walk with sticks in front of the car measuring, but Kim still drove carefully on the slippery road.

After about half an hour they could see the Ferris wheel looming ahead, and signs began to appear. NORTH SHORE SUMMER FAIR 1 MILE the first one proclaimed in bright-green Brush Script font (according to Pippa). A little while later a sign said ½ MILE. Now that they were close, Kim kept expecting to see others driving toward the fair, but there were no other cars on the road. Perhaps the heavy rain the day before had scared everyone away.

As she rounded a bend in the road, she spotted a sign with an arrow pointing to the parking lot, but there was no dry ground visible, only a square space full of water like a sad, muddy wading pool. She flicked on her turn signal (she was still a very safe driver even when there were no other drivers around) and headed for a spot at the far end of the lot. "Looks like we have the place to ourselves," she said to Toby, but just then Toby jabbed his finger out and wailed, "No!" He was pointing toward the Ferris wheel, which he had just noticed wasn't moving. The little chairs rocked back and forth in the breeze, but the wheel that held them wasn't spinning.

When they got to the base of the Ferris wheel, they discovered that someone had hung a chain across the bottom of it with a handwritten sign that said CLOSED DUE TO RAIN. Now there would be no rides—and no chance to look for a house from the air.

They made the best of the afternoon anyway. There was almost no one at the fair besides the people who'd been hired to work there. This meant there were no lines. The Fitzgerald-Trouts decided to spend the money they had set aside for the Ferris wheel at the games tent, and they wandered from game to game without having to wait for anyone else to play.

Toby tried a game where you pulled a plastic duck out of a pond and looked on its bottom to see if you got an X that marked a win. He was hoping to win a pet snail, but he didn't get an X. Kim and Pippa tried throwing beanbags into buckets, but they both had terrible aim. Kimo didn't want to waste any more money on games, but then Kim, who had always said that Kimo was unnaturally strong, convinced him to have a go at a game where you swung a large hammer down and tried to hit a spot so hard that it rang a bell. Kimo lifted the hammer and swung it down and rang the bell in one try. Everyone laughed with surprise as the words MEGA MUSCLES appeared in flashing lights. Kimo's strength was now official. He picked out a stuffed purple octopus as his prize.

Penny saw the octopus and stretched out her hands, dropping her doll on the ground in the process. She gave a loud squeal of delight: "Mine!"

"Did you hear that?" Pippa was as proud as any mother has ever been on hearing her baby's first word.

"Wow!" said Kimo.

"You did it!" Kim kissed Penny on the head, then scooped up the abandoned doll.

Toby was grinning and Penny, sensing her siblings' pleasure, tried it again. "Mine! Mine! Mine!" Kimo put the octopus in the baby's hands. The creature was almost as big as Penny and anyone looking at her from far away would have thought the purple animal was strangling the baby with its arms and not the other way around. "Mine!" Penny announced one more time, with relish. The purple octopus was already damp with her drool.

"Lunchtime," said Toby.

"My humble stomach could use some food," said Kim, recalling the digestive biscuit package. Kimo pointed the way to a massive circus tent where all the food vendors had little stalls set up and were selling foods from around the world. With so few customers, the vendors were eager to sell their food before it went bad.

"Ten cents for a plate of sushi!" the sushi chef cried out.

Not to be outsold, the Greek food vendor yelled, "Five cents for a plate of stuffed grape leaves!"

"Two cents for curry!" the curry cook called.

"A penny for pork chops!" the pork chop salesman shouted.

Out of the blue, the pizza maker hollered, "Free samples! Over here!"

The other vendors must have known their food would not last long and they must have wanted someone to appreciate it, because suddenly all of them chimed in, saying they would give their food away. Free samples.

The Fitzgerald-Trouts had their pick of delicacies. They wandered from stall to stall tasting whatever appealed to them. From Hawaii, they had a soup called saimin with tiny pink fish cakes in it. From Korea, they had barbecued meat. From Sri Lanka, they had little piles of noodles called string hoppers covered with coconut curry. From Mexico, there was fish cooked in lime juice. From

Portugal, there were pastries called malasadas that were rolled in sugar. From Italy, there was a frozen dessert like ice cream, only it was made from shaved almonds. They ate and ate, going from country to country.

They didn't realize how full they were because before their stomachs could register it, they had begun to eat the next thing. Then Toby said he wanted to eat something from "Chungary," and Pippa laughed and said, "Chungary isn't a country."

"Yes it is," said Toby, though suddenly he wasn't sure.

"China is a country," Kim offered, "and Hungary is a country. Did you mean one of those?"

"Maybe," said Toby, and Pippa said rudely, "Kim needs to put *Teach Toby geography* on that to-do list of hers."

"I know geography," said Toby.

"Oh yeah," said Pippa. "Is Chile a country? Is Turkey?"

"No," said Toby. "Those are foods."

"Ha," said Pippa. "They're foods *and* countries. I told you you don't know geography."

"Do too," insisted Toby, clutching Goldie's jar to his heart. "I know all about Tobyworld." The minute he said it, he wished that he hadn't. Tobyworld was a secret place and he knew he shouldn't have breathed a word about it.

"Tobyworld?" Pippa snorted. "Don't tell me.... It's a country ruled by a goldfish." Deeply regretting having told her, Toby swung his fist at Pippa, but the girl leapt out of the way.

"Pippa! Apologize!" said Kim, but it was too late. Toby had turned on his heel and was running away.

"She didn't mean it," said Kimo, then he turned to Pippa. "Tell him you didn't mean it."

"I *did* mean it," said Pippa. "He's obsessed with that fish."

"You're just jealous," Toby shouted back at her. Kim called out to him, "Where are you going?"

"To Tobyworld!" he yelled. He was sprinting

now, and Goldie was sloshing in his jar, riding the waves of Toby's fury.

"Let him blow off steam," said Kimo. "We'll find him in a little while." Kim looked nervous, but then thought that since there was no one else at the fair they would be able to find Toby easily once he had had time to be alone and cool down.

The argument had taken long enough for all the older children to realize that they weren't hungry anymore. "You could try being nicer," Kimo said to Pippa as they left the food stalls.

"Yeah, yeah," said Pippa, who knew that Kimo was right. After she hurt Toby's feelings, she always felt rotten.

They headed for a large tent where tables were set up with different products for sale. Each table featured a recent invention that some company on the island was trying to sell. Each table also had a salesperson waiting to describe the wonder of these items. The children wandered past the booths, hearing about pumps that removed salt from seawater and composting toilets and brizzill bug zappers. After their recent encounter with the cloud of brizzill bugs, Kimo was interested in the zappers. He stood at the booth scratching his bug bites as the salesman talked about the terrible brizzill bug infestation that had overtaken the island. "Worst bug season anyone has ever seen," said the man as he turned on the zapper, which looked like nothing but a bright blue light. The salesman touched the light with a raw sausage, and the zapper went *ZAAAPPP!* Then the salesman showed Kimo that the tip of the sausage was cooked. This was what would happen to a bug that flew into the zapper. Kimo shook his head. It seemed very cruel to cook a bug just because you didn't want it to bite you.

Unsettled by the idea, Kimo started for the next table, where a man stood speaking into a bullhorn that projected his voice with a metallic screech: "GOT BUG TROUBLES?" Kimo scratched his bites again and answered, "Yeah, I do."

"Everyone does these days," said the man, who

was wearing a green jumpsuit with a long metal zipper up the front. He put down the bullhorn and reached for a stack of business cards. "Call Professor Mumby," the man said brightly. "She can help."

"How does she help?" asked Kimo. "What's her invention?"

"You have to ask her," said the man, offering Kimo one of the cards, which had a phone number on it.

"Mine," said Penny, who was in Kimo's arms, still holding her octopus.

"Not for you," Kimo said to the baby, then he turned to the man and said, "Thanks." He slid the card into his pocket.

Pippa was also collecting business cards and pamphlets. She had once invented a contraption to keep bloodsucking iguanas off their car and was taken with the many other inventions on display. She was racing from table to table, trying to look at all of them. She began to imagine how someday when she was older she might sell her iguana contraptions at a fair like this one. She imagined her picture on a pamphlet next to a drawing of a bloodsucking iguana with a big X through it. The idea thrilled her.

Kim was wandering the booths, caught up in imaginings of her own. She was thinking that she might happen upon a booth that sold a do-it-yourself home construction kit. Was there such a thing? If there was, where would they construct their home? She was about to tell her idea to Kimo and Pippa when someone came up behind her and poked her between the shoulders, saying, "Help."

She turned to find Toby bouncing from foot to foot with excitement. "A contest," he told her. There was nothing Toby loved more than a contest. "I need you to write my name." Toby had learned in kindergarten how to write his name, but since the summer had begun he'd forgotten.

"What's the contest?" asked Kim.

"Just a contest," said Toby, who was too excited to explain himself.

"What's the prize?"

"Come," said Toby, pulling Kim's hand and dragging her toward a far corner of the tent. Kim called to the others and they all followed.

What they found at the far end of that tent was a contest that exceeded their wildest expectations. The prize wasn't a pet snail or a stuffed purple octopus. The prize was so much more: an enormous, fully outfitted, brand-new motorboat with tall fishing poles sticking off the back. It sat on a metal trailer with two wheels so that the boat could be driven to the ocean. There was a big captain's chair that faced a large instrument panel. It had a huge silver steering wheel. It had a little door that opened onto a ladder that led down to a small cabin. From the photographs taped to the side of the boat, they could tell that inside the cabin there were two wide bunks, a folding wooden table, a little kitchen, and even a small bathroom.

In other words, sitting in front of them was the answer to their dreams. It was the number one thing on Kim's to-do list: a house. Actually, something even better than a house. A boat-house from which they could drop a fishing line and catch their dinner.

The five Fitzgerald-Trouts stood there looking up at the boat in reverent awe, until the silence was broken by a single word: "Mine." They all turned to look at the baby, but it was Toby who had spoken.

CHAPTER
7

They wrote their names on slips of paper and shoved them through the slot in a tall cardboard box that stood beside the boat. Each of them, that is, except Toby, who asked Kim to write his name, and Penny, who had no idea they were entering her in a contest at all.

Toby crunched up his slip of paper so that it would be easier to grab and slid it into the box, then he pressed his eye to the hole to see how many other slips of paper were in there. But the inside of the box was too dark for him to see anything.

"Maybe if we shake it we can tell," said Kimo, who was kneeling down to pick up the box. But before he could lift it, a voice called out to him, "Put that down."

They turned to see a man in a blue-and-white sailor suit hustling toward them. "Don't mess with that."

Kimo did as he was told and set the box down as Kim turned to the man, asking, "Are you in charge of the contest?" She had noticed that the sailor suit had a logo stitched on the square collar that matched the logo on the side of the boat. GRIMSTONE, it said in bright blue letters.

"Sure am," offered the man, who was also wearing a fisherman's cap and a black eye patch. He had a pipe clamped between his teeth. Kim felt bad for him. He looked like someone straight out of an advertisement for fish sticks, and it seemed to her that he must have been forced to wear the silly costume by whoever owned the company. But then he held out his hand for her to shake. "Captain Clayton Grimstone. Sole proprietor, Grimstone Fishing Vessels," he said. Kim shook the man's hand, realizing that if he owned the company he must not have been forced to wear the silly outfit; the outfit was his own idea.

"When are you drawing the winner?" Kim asked.

" 'One o'clock sharp. Rain or shine.' " This was said by Kimo, who was reading the rules of the contest printed on a sign above the cardboard box.

"Actually," said the captain, "that's not accurate."

"What do you mean?" asked Kimo. "It says it right here."

"There aren't many people at the fair so I'm going to wait till later this afternoon when the roads are completely dry and more people are here. Then I'll draw the winner."

"But that's not right," said Pippa.

"You can't do that," agreed Kimo.

"Certainly can," countered the captain. "It's my contest."

"It says rain or shine," Pippa asserted. "It says one o'clock sharp."

"It's one o'clock now," said Toby, who had only a vague sense of the time but hoped that he was right.

The captain looked at his watch, and they all saw that it was after one o'clock.

"You promised," said Pippa, her brown freckles igniting on her cheeks. "You gave your word." She pointed to the sign hanging above the box.

"But there's no one here," the captain whined, and Kim wondered—not for the first time—why grown-ups were always whining.

"You have to draw now," said Pippa, "unless you're comfortable with people knowing that the word of Captain Clayton Grimstone isn't worth the paper it's printed on." Pippa crossed her arms over her chest and glared at the captain, who nervously chomped on the stem of his pipe. The three other children took their cue from Pippa and crossed their arms and glared at him too. Even the baby, who was still holding the octopus, managed to look indignant.

"Oh, what the hay," said the captain. "What do I care? It's a tax write-off anyway." The children had no idea what he meant, but they sensed that they had won as the captain lifted the box's lid and closed the eye that wasn't covered by the patch. He bent over and reached far into the bottom of the box, where the slips of paper sat with the contestants' names on them. It was entirely possible that no one had entered the contest except the five Fitzgerald-Trouts. After all, there was absolutely no one else at the fair on that rain-soaked day. Knowing this, each of them held his or her breath. Each hoped against hope that he or she would be the one whose slip of paper was chosen.

The captain drew the winning slip and squinted at it but said nothing. He was having trouble reading with just the one uncovered eye. He slid off his eye patch, squinted again, then pronounced, "Kimo Fitzgerald-Trout."

It was a moment before anyone said anything. Finally Kimo shook his head and whispered, "I won?"

"You did," answered Kim and Pippa in unison. Kimo shook his head again. He was dazed by his good fortune, dazed by the good fortune of all of them because, of course, they would all share the boat. He knew that. So did Kim and Pippa, who let out whoops of joy. Pippa spun on her heel, which made baby Penny giggle. The boat—with the fishing poles and the captain's chair and the silver wheel and the ladder down to the cabin that held two bunks, a table, a kitchen, and a bathroom—was theirs! All theirs!

But Toby, who didn't see it this way at all, burst into tears. "It was my contest," he cried. "I found it and it was mine. I shouldn't have told any of you about it!"

"Don't be mad," said Kimo. "The boat belongs to all of us." He grabbed Toby by the waist and lifted him off his feet. "We'll share it."

Toby was kicking his legs in the air as Kimo raised him up over his head. "You can't have it," Toby was shouting at Kimo. "You can't!"

Hearing this, Kim suddenly thought that maybe what Toby said was true. Maybe they couldn't have the boat. It had all happened so quickly and so easily that a part of her couldn't quite believe it. Had they really won a floating house? Kim turned to the captain and asked the dangerous question, "Is the boat really his?"

"Certainly is," said the captain. "He can take it away whenever he wants. He just has to hitch that trailer to a car and drag it to the ocean." The captain pointed to the metal trailer that soon would be bolted to the back of their little green car. Then he added, "He also needs to show me ID proving that he's eighteen years old." Kim swallowed hard and felt her hands begin to shake. The captain frowned at her. "He *is* eighteen years old, isn't he?"

Kim didn't answer. Kimo, who had been holding Toby aloft and dancing, stopped. He certainly was not eighteen years old and any adult who thought he was had no idea about children. Before Kimo could say a word, Pippa blurted out, "Are you crazy? He just turned eleven."

"Well," the captain said with a shrug, "if he's only eleven and he wants to claim the boat, he needs a parent to sign for it." And with that word, *parent*, the five Fitzgerald-Trouts felt their victory sliding away. They had no parent who would do such a thing. They had no parent who could be trusted.

CHAPTER
8

Gurgle, gurgle went the little green car as it lurched over the potholed road heading away from the flooded fairgrounds and back toward the south shore of the island. Kim had her foot pressed to the gas and was driving as quickly as she dared. She and the others had a destination in mind and they were not going to let anything slow their progress.

Back at the fair, when the children had realized they could not take the boat themselves, they immediately began searching for another way to claim it. They all knew that asking a parent was out of the question. Even Penny, at her young age, must have understood they had no parent who could be relied upon. But Kim was convinced the solution to their troubles lay in the boat and she was not going to walk away from it without putting up a fight. So she had stomped her foot and turned her imperious gaze on the captain, saying, "Where does it say a parent has to sign for the boat?"

"In the fine print," the captain answered, pointing to the sign above the cardboard box. So Kim had stepped closer and read the fine print on the sign. This is what it said:

Winners under eighteen years of age may claim their prize with the signature of a parent or guardian.

"It says a parent *or* guardian!" Kim's voice was triumphant.

"I suppose it does," said the captain, who then added, "Certainly." It was a word he said a lot and it made him sound very *un*certain.

"What's a guardian?" Toby was hopping from foot to foot. He had been very angry that Kimo had won the boat, and he was secretly excited that Kimo was going to have trouble claiming it.

"A guardian is someone who takes care of you when your parents can't," Kimo answered.

"Do you have a guardian?" Captain Grimstone queried them.

Kim and Kimo looked at each other, measuring their thoughts on the thread that ran between them and realizing that they were thinking exactly the same thing. Kim nodded at the captain. "We have someone who feeds us and gives us clean clothes and watches TV with us. Does that qualify?"

"Certainly," said the captain, again sounding uncertain.

"Good," said Kim. "We'll be back in a few hours." That was when she'd hustled them all off toward the wet parking lot to begin their cross-island trek. They took a route over Mount Muldoon, where the roads were high enough to be dry, and as Kim drove, Kimo explained to the younger Fitzgerald-Trouts that they were going to the laundromat to talk to Mr. Knuckles. After all, he had let them sit in his chairs for as many hours as they wanted, watching his TV and eating chocolate bars from the broken vending machine while their clothes went round and round. According to the captain, this qualified Mr. Knuckles as the children's guardian. Kim and Kimo were both certain that he could be convinced to drive back across the island and sign on the dotted line so that they could claim the boat.

But when they pulled into a parking spot near the laundromat, they found the doors closed and the shop dark. They had never seen it like this before. The laundromat was known to be open twenty-four hours a day, seven days a week. Its shuttered appearance was as shocking to the children as if, one day, the sun had decided not to rise.

The Fitzgerald-Trouts (including the goldfish in the jar in Toby's arms) pressed against the laundromat's windows, trying to get a look inside. But none of them could see much of anything except the hulking dark shapes of the washers and dryers that lined the walls. What could have happened? They turned away from the glass and stood with their backs to the laundromat, staring into the distance. Pippa was delighted to see a dozen mynahs wading in a nearby puddle, splashing their wings in the dirty water, treating themselves to an oily and gritty birdbath. Since no one was saying anything, she idly offered, "Maybe Mr. Knuckles is upstairs taking a bath."

"Why would he do that?" Kimo asked. Pippa shrugged, but Toby said, "He'd do it because he got dirty."

"He's never closed the laundromat before," Kimo said, frowning.

"Maybe he's never been this dirty." Toby tried logic.

"But he goes off for hours at a time—to buy groceries, to walk on the beach with his metal detector, to get new tattoos—and he never closes the laundromat. He just leaves it open and lets people do their laundry. Everything is automatic anyway." Kimo was trying to explain to Toby just why Toby's logic was flawed.

But Kim was stuck on the thing Pippa had first said. "What do you mean, 'upstairs'?" she asked.

Pippa shrugged and straightened her glasses. "Can you hold Penny? My arms are tired."

"Certainly," said Kim—she had picked up the word from the captain—"but you have to answer the question. What do you mean by 'upstairs'?"

Pippa lifted the baby out of the sling and handed her to Kim. "You know how Mr. Knuckles has that apartment...."

"He does?" Kim didn't know about any apartment.

"Indeed," said Pippa. "There's a set of metal stairs outside the back of the laundromat and I've seen him go up them and come back down holding a cup of coffee and a peanut butter sandwich. So he must have some kind of kitchen up there, at the very least."

"He shouldn't eat peanut butter," said Toby, who had been taught in kindergarten about the dangers of nut allergies. This was the kind of off-point comment that drove Kim crazy, but she was sticking to her promise to be nicer to her little brother so she ignored him and stepped out from under the awning. She pointed at the windows of whatever was above the laundromat. "Is that the place?"

"Indeed," Pippa said again.

"Maybe he's up there now," said Kimo, slapping a brizzill bug that had landed on his arm. "Let's find the stairs."

They started off toward the back of the laundromat, where they found a weedy lot strewn with litter. The sky was clear and the sun shone down on them as they picked their way through the towers of old tires and rusty metal canisters until they came to the foot of the metal staircase. Kimo stopped and turned to Kim. "We're sure about this?" Kim understood why he was hesitating. The Fitzgerald-Trouts were very private children who were used to relying only on themselves. It was difficult for them to ask anyone else for help.

"We need a home," said Kim. "We can't keep living in the car."

"You're right," Kimo said, remembering how easy life had been at the cabin on Wabo Point before his father had locked them out. With a grunt, he started up the stairs, taking them two at a time. When he reached the top, he knocked politely on the door.

It took a while for anything to happen. They could hear someone moving on the other side of it, shuffling, shuffling closer to the door, which, at long last, swung open. There, in the dark hallway, wearing nothing but a pair of baggy sweatpants and a small tank top (so small that it revealed his many colorful tattoos), stood Mr. Knuckles. He looked dazed, as if he had not seen sunlight for a very long time.

"Hey, you…children." He blinked. "Hey, you… Fitzgerald-Trouts…" His voice trailed off. He seemed to Kim to have lost the will to finish the sentence. This was confirmed when he turned suddenly from the door and started back down the short hallway of the apartment. The children, who were crowded on the little landing at the top of the stairs, looked at one another.

"I guess we shouldn't have asked for help," said Kimo.

"But we haven't asked anything yet." Kim was confused and more than a little hurt. She cooed to the baby, who was wiggling in her arms. She rocked her gently, as if being nice to the baby might take away some of the feelings of rejection that she herself was feeling.

"There's something wrong," said Pippa. She had made a decision and was heading down the dark hallway, following Mr. Knuckles's retreat. She followed him around a corner into a dark room, where he was heading for a couch that sat near a window with tightly closed blue shutters. Pippa looked around and saw that the floor of the room was covered by a carpet made of dried and braided maha leaves. Maps of the island hung on one wall of the bedroom (Mr. Knuckles had a passion for island history) and on another an intricate mural was painted. It looked like it had been drawn by the same person who had designed the tattoos that covered Mr. Knuckles. Pippa stared at the beautiful design until she noticed that Mr. Knuckles was climbing onto the couch and turning his back to her. Suddenly she felt embarrassed. Being in the room with Mr. Knuckles was like running into your teacher at the beach wearing a bikini and eating an ice-cream cone. Nobody wanted that to happen.

She stood there a moment, thinking what to do. Should she leave? Then she remembered the time at the beach when she'd tamed a seal. It had taken a long time to get close to that seal; she had had to talk to it quietly and walk toward it slowly so that it wouldn't slip back into the water and swim away. Now she decided to treat Mr. Knuckles not like a teacher she'd run into at the beach but like a seal. She began to walk toward the couch, taking the same slow time she had taken with the seal and saying the same quiet things she had said on the beach: "Here, boy, here, boy, it's okay, it's okay...." Mr. Knuckles didn't slide back into the water and swim away, but he might have if there had been a nearby ocean. Instead he just lay there with his back to the freckled little girl.

The others had come down the hallway and were crowded in the doorway of the dark room. They watched as Pippa slowly tried to tame Mr. Knuckles. When she was at last standing over him as he lay on the couch, Pippa carefully reached out a hand and touched the man's shoulder. "What's wrong, Mr. Knuckles?"

He didn't answer, but he did roll over to look at her, and that was when Pippa saw—in the dim light coming through the blue shutters—that Mr. Knuckles had a brand-new tattoo poking out from under his tank top. The tattoo was of a large red heart torn down the middle so that it seemed to be breaking in two. The heart had the name ASHA tattooed across it in black letters.

"Mr. Knuckles," Pippa said gently, "have you had your heart broken?"

Mr. Knuckles answered with a single word: "Asha..."

"Oh, Mr. Knuckles." Pippa bent down and

hugged the man with her fragile little arms. "I'm so sorry...." Mr. Knuckles began to cry.

None of them knew what to do to repair a broken heart. Kim thought that they should respond to Mr. Knuckles's broken heart the way they would respond to any other physical problem—a flu, a stomachache, a snake bite—with a cup of hot tea. This was something she had read about in books like *The Secret Garden*, where sickly characters were given lots of cups of tea. Since there was a grocery store next to the laundromat, Kimo and Toby offered to go back downstairs to buy the necessary tea while Penny played on the carpet and Pippa and Kim tried to coax Mr. Knuckles out of the room.

The first step was to open the shutters and turn on the light. That was easy. The second step was to engage Mr. Knuckles in conversation. This was not so easy. Mr. Knuckles, who had stopped crying, had also completely clammed up. He wouldn't say a word and wouldn't answer any of their questions. After about a dozen questions Pippa happened to ask, "Who's Asha?" That was the key. Suddenly a tidal wave of words came rushing from Mr. Knuckles's mouth. Asha, the brilliant. Asha, the beautiful. Asha, the brave. Asha, they learned, worked at the grocery store (in fact, Kimo and Toby were buying tea from her at that very moment). She had been in the habit of doing her laundry once a week at the laundromat after her grocery store shift. She would bring Mr. Knuckles day-old doughnuts and they would sit and watch TV together and chat about island things while her laundry sloshed in the suds. Slowly this routine had grown more frequent, and eventually she seemed to be coming by to do her laundry every day. One afternoon Mr. Knuckles noticed that she had put a perfectly clean pile of T-shirts into the washing machine. That was when he'd realized—with a surge of joy—that the laundry was just an excuse and what Asha really wanted was to visit with him. He had promptly asked her out on a date and she had said yes.

After that, Asha had been Mr. Knuckles's girlfriend. Their relationship had lasted for several happy months during which time they had eaten many day-old doughnuts. One afternoon Mr. Knuckles had been combing the beach with his metal detector and the machine had made its buzzing noise that usually meant he had stumbled across a bottle cap or an old hanger, but when he'd stooped down and pawed through the sand he had found a small gold ring with a bright green stone set into it. It seemed to him like a sign and he decided then and there to ask Asha to marry him. For days he had paced around the laundromat, practicing all the ways to ask her. Should he get down on his knees? Should he sing a song? Should he hire a plane and write his question in the sky? If he did, what would it say? He had written down a hundred different versions of the question. Finally he settled on putting the ring inside a day-old doughnut. She would bite the doughnut and find the ring and then he would ask her.

But it didn't happen that way. Instead the story took a darker turn. Mr. Knuckles groaned and shifted on the couch. "Tuesday she come into laundromat. Ring already in doughnut, but she no look happy. She look sad." (Mr. Knuckles was fluent in the native language of the island, but when he spoke English he sometimes left out words.) Before he could offer her the doughnut, Asha announced to Mr. Knuckles that it was over. The manager of the frozen food section had asked her out on a date and she was going.

"Her heart as cold as frozen steak." Mr. Knuckles groaned again and gave his new tattoo a tender poke.

"Oh, Mr. Knuckles." Pippa sighed. And that was when Kim saw a shocking sight: A tear had formed in the corner of Pippa's eye. A *tear*. All Kim had been thinking about as Mr. Knuckles had told his story was how they were going to get him up out of bed and back to the fairgrounds to sign his name for Kimo's boat. In other words, she had been thinking selfish thoughts. Now she felt ashamed. Pippa—the fiercest and most temperamental of them all—had actually been listening to the story and truly felt sad for Mr. Knuckles.

"You'll never win her back this way," Pippa said, shaking her head. "You need to get up and get control of yourself. If you don't, the frozen food manager is going to get all the day-old doughnuts from now on."

"He probably get them anyway." Mr. Knuckles could not be cheered up.

And that was when Kim struck upon an idea that would help both Mr. Knuckles and the five Fitzgerald-Trouts. "I think," said Kim carefully, "if she saw you doing something noble, something to help someone else, Asha might just love you again...."

"You think?" Mr. Knuckles asked.

"Yes," said Kim.

"What I do?"

"There's something you could do to help five children who are in need," Kim said, and Pippa—who suddenly understood Kim's plan—looked at her older sister with admiration. "If you helped

those five children," Kim continued, "they would tell Asha what you had done and her cold heart might thaw and she might love you again."

It was a lot of hypotheticals, but Mr. Knuckles didn't seem to care. "Tell me what to do," he said, and he sat up on the couch.

This time when they pulled into the wet parking lot at the fairgrounds they saw that the Ferris wheel was turning and people were riding on it, but that didn't matter to the Fitzgerald-Trouts. They were focused on a greater prize: Kimo's boat with the fishing poles and the captain's chair and the silver wheel and the ladder down to the cabin that held two bunks, a table, a kitchen, and a bathroom. They hurried out of the car and grabbed Penny from her car seat. Mr. Knuckles—who had followed

them across the island on his motorcycle—parked and took off his helmet, then they all rushed across the parking lot. Amazingly the floodwater on the north shore of the island had completely receded, and the fairgrounds were almost dry. Mud squished pleasantly between the children's toes as they ran to the far end of the tent to claim their boat.

But when they got there, the boat was gone.

There was no sign of it. And no sign of the trailer. The only evidence there had ever been a boat or a contest was the cardboard box with the sign hanging over it.

The five Fitzgerald-Trouts and Mr. Knuckles stood shaking their heads, staring at the spot where the boat had once stood, wondering what could have happened.

"The captain must have taken it somewhere to store it for us while we went to get our guardian." This was Kimo, the most practical of the group.

"Maybe he put in ocean for you," Mr. Knuckles agreed with Kimo.

But Kim and Pippa shared a look of unease. Something wasn't right. "We've got to find the captain," they said, almost in unison.

"Let's spread out across the fairgrounds. There still aren't very many people," Kim said. "If the captain is here, we'll find him." They decided to split up into groups of two, and they were standing in a small circle, doing rock-paper-scissors to determine who would go with whom, when they heard a voice behind them: "Oh, here you are...."

They turned and saw Captain Grimstone. "I went to get a coffee," he said. He was holding a paper coffee cup in his hand. "Everything okay?"

"Where's the boat?" Kim narrowed her eyes and stuck out her chin, threatening.

The captain shrugged and said, "No idea."

"What do you mean?" Kim's heart was beating fast, her body thrumming with fury. "How can you have no idea where it is?"

"Your father signed for it," said the captain. "You'll have to ask him."

"Our father?" Kim blinked and shook her head. Just saying the word *father* made her feel enraged. "What father?"

"Johnny Trout," the captain said. "He came to claim the boat. I thought he was bringing it to you."

"He took my boat?" This was Kimo, sputtering with disbelief. "You let him take it?"

"He *is* your father, isn't he?" asked the captain. And Kimo reluctantly nodded. Johnny Trout was Kimo's father, his terrible, terrible father.

"I gave him the boat and the deed with your name on it."

"My name on what?" asked Kimo, his face darkening.

"The deed," said the captain. "It's a piece of paper that says you own the boat."

"What good is that if he doesn't *have* the boat?" demanded Kim just as Penny began to cry.

"She can tell we're upset," Pippa said.

"She drop octopus," said Mr. Knuckles.

Toby picked up the toy and returned it to the baby, thinking how glad he was that in Toby-world there was absolutely no such thing as a parent.

"I thought you'd sent your father," the captain said to Kimo, "seeing as you needed a parent to sign." The captain took a sip of his coffee then looked startled. "Ouch," he said. "I burned my mouth."

"Serves you right," said Pippa, whose freckles were seething. "Giving away Kimo's boat."

"You need to learn some manners." Captain Grimstone frowned at Pippa, peeling back the coffee lid and blowing on the hot liquid to cool it down.

"Oh, and I guess that's good manners," said Pippa, "blowing on your coffee? I bet that's just what the queen of England does when her coffee is too hot!"

"Stop it," said Kimo, who had larger concerns. "Where did Johnny Trout take my boat?" Kimo was beginning to feel the first bubbles of rage, like water coming to a boil in a pot.

"I told you," said the captain. "I've got no idea where that boat is."

"Johnny go Wabo Point," said Mr. Knuckles. "He got cabin there."

The other children knew that Mr. Knuckles was right, and that the next step must be to go to Wabo Point and confront Johnny, forcing him to show them the deed that proved the boat was Kimo's. Then they would demand that he give the boat back. Without a word, they turned and started away from the captain.

They had walked only a few feet when Kimo thought of one last question. He turned back and said, "How did Johnny Trout know that I had won?"

"Didn't you tell him?" asked the captain.

"No," said Kimo. "I would never do that."

Kimo's heart had hardened against his father since the night he'd been locked out of the cabin.

"Maybe someone who works at the fair told him," the captain was guessing. "They announced over the loudspeaker that you had won. Maybe someone phoned him."

"Unbelievable," said Kimo, then he added, "Who would do such a thing?" It was a rhetorical question, of course. He didn't expect any of them to answer. And none of them did.

They drove in silence along the coastal road that led to the forest. Mr. Knuckles wasn't following them anymore. He hadn't offered his help, and they hadn't asked for it. Unless he had the nose of a basset-hound ninja, Mr. Knuckles was not going to be any better at finding the boat than they were. Kim was thinking this very thought and muttering to herself the new number one thing on her to-do list—"find the boat, find the boat, find the boat"—as she turned the little green car down the dirt road that led to the edge of the Sakahatchi Forest.

The children began to see signs that read PRO-CEED AT YOUR OWN RISK, and Kim did just that, proceeding cautiously and slowly, but proceeding nonetheless. They all knew they would see nine of these signs before they reached the beginning of the forest and the even smaller road that headed through it and led to Wabo Point. It was a road that they themselves had created by driving back and forth between Wabo and the dirt road during the time they had lived in Johnny's cabin. It was also a dangerous road that had to be driven with the windows up because otherwise bloodsucking iguanas would attack the car and its inhabitants. (Pippa's spiky iguana contraptions were glued to the car to stop the attacks.)

When they saw the ninth sign—PROCEED WITH CAUTION—the children instinctively began to roll up their windows, preparing for the bumpy ride through the forest of iguanas. They were surprised when Kim hit the brakes on the car.

"What are you doing?" This was Kimo, who hadn't been following the thread of Kim's thoughts. He had been stewing in his anger against his father.

"The road is getting narrow," Kim said. "Give me the binoculars."

Pippa, who was wearing them around her neck, took them off and handed them to her older sister. "What are you looking for?"

"Tire tracks," said Kim, who had the binoculars pressed to her eyes and was scanning the road. "Aha!" she cried, and pointed toward tracks in the road made by two tires. "See how far apart they are?"

"Indeed," said Pippa, who could see that the tire tracks were much farther apart than a regular car's tire tracks would be.

"The boat trailer," Kimo said, picking up the thread of Kim's thinking.

"See how they stop," said Kim. "See how the trailer couldn't drive any farther because it didn't fit between the trees?" They looked to where Kim was pointing and saw that exactly where the road narrowed and went up and over the roots of two closely planted trees, the trailer's tire tracks made a U-turn and came back.

"The boat on the trailer never made it to Wabo Point," Kim said. "It wouldn't fit."

Kimo clenched his fist and punched it at the air, as if boxing an invisible enemy. "Where is it?" he shouted angrily.

"It could be anywhere," said Pippa.

"If he took it," said Kim, "he wants to use it. So he's going to launch it into the ocean."

"But where?" Pippa moaned.

"It's an island," said Kimo, trying to regain his composure. He didn't like to feel this angry. "But he can't just launch it anywhere."

"Not from a mountain," said Toby very seriously.

"Not from rocks." This was Pippa.

"Not from a spot where the surf is high," Kim added.

"Right," said Kimo. "Wherever he launches it, there has to be a calm beach with a road down to it."

"Let's make a list of places like that," said Kim. "I bet we can name every single one." It was true; they could. They were islanders, after all, and they knew every nook and cranny of their home. As they drove back to town, they wrote a list of places where the boat could be launched. The only paper they had was their report cards, handed to them by their teachers on the last day of school a few weeks before. Kimo found them crammed in the glove compartment and got them out, flattening them with his hand on the dashboard.

"I didn't know we had paper," said Pippa, who had been longing for something to doodle on.

"Here," said Kimo, giving them to her. They were printed on both sides but had wide margins.

Pippa put down the words *Boat Launch List* in a spot on the margin, just beside her B-minus grade in penmanship and the teacher's comment: *Pippa needs to learn to write in standard cursive; too often she invents her own style of lettering.*

"Now," said Kim, "if you had a boat, where would you launch it?"

The Fitzgerald-Trouts began to shout out names—Tender Beach, Pigeonholes, Roolie Poolie flats, Proud Mama's, Reef Walker Bay, Wa'a's Marsh, Poi Pounders—and Pippa wrote them down. As they listed places, Kimo realized that all of them were reachable from the coastal road that ran around the island. They could use the road as their route, stopping at each place on the list, looking for the trailer's tracks and asking beachgoers or surfers if they had seen the boat. Everyone agreed this was a good plan.

They finished the list just as the sun was beginning to set behind the shops and stores of the downtown. "If you drive fast we can get to Pea Tree before dark," said Kimo. "Maybe this will be easy—maybe the boat is there."

The boat wasn't there, but they decided to stay for the night anyway. As long as it didn't rain, a couple of them could sleep on the beach and the car would be more comfortable for the others. As darkness descended, the air grew thick with brizzill bugs, but the children collected enough brush to get their old campfire going again and that kept the bugs away. They sat around it (on logs they had long ago arranged in a circle), eating beef jerky and toasting marshmallows while they talked about the day's events. So much had happened since they'd woken that morning in the flooded house. Kimo wanted to talk about the moment when he'd learned that he'd won the boat. Kim indulged him, and Toby didn't argue. He was trying very hard not to be mad that he'd lost the contest, especially now that it seemed the boat would never belong to any of them. Kim kept going through the descriptions of all the people they'd met at the fair—the sushi chef, the Greek food vendor, and everyone else—wondering which of them had called Johnny Trout to tell him about the boat.

"Who exactly is Johnny Trout's henchman?" she asked, using a word from *The Nosy Ninja*.

Pippa wasn't interested in any of this. She was playing with Penny in the sand, tickling the baby's tummy and talking to her about poor Mr. Knuckles and his broken heart. Why had Asha so suddenly broken up with him?

When the fire burned down and they were too tired to collect more wood, they poured sand over the logs to put out the flames completely. Then they brushed their teeth and went to sleep. They had a long list of places to visit the next morning.

The sun was still a pink blur rising out of the ocean when the Fitzgerald-Trouts arrived at Stickleback Ledge, the first spot on the list. They combed the beach, searching for the trailer's tracks and asking beachgoers if they had seen a brand-new Grimstone fishing boat. No one was able to give them any information. Before moving on to the next place on the list, they decided to have a swim. After that, they picked some pomelo fruits from the trees that bordered the beach,

and then Pippa found a sugarcane field so they had to eat some of that too. Before they knew it, the morning was spent.

There were eighty-seven places on their list and it might have taken them only four or five days to visit them all—searching for tracks and asking about the boat. The problem was that every place on the list was just as much fun as Stickleback had been. Every beach they stopped at was beautiful in its own way; some had reefs full of colorful fish and some had sandbars that made the water so shallow you could walk straight out into the ocean for miles. There were surfing spots and sand-boarding spots and places with cliffs that were perfect for jumping. There were blowholes and tide pools, sand dunes and old sunken wrecks. And every spot had things to eat. At Tender Beach there were thickets of guava bushes filled with the delicious pink fruit. Across the street from Lala's, there was a pineapple field. The parking lot of Proud Mama's had the best shaved-ice truck on the whole island, and Do-Gooder Bay was perfect for walla-willi fishing.

The children were happy wherever they were, so it was hard to convince themselves to pile their salty, sticky bodies back into the car and drive to somewhere else.

At night they camped, and they sat around the campfire promising one another that the next day they would be more efficient. They would pick less fruit, they would spend less time swimming, they would surf less and sand-board less and fish less. But then the morning would come and it would be hard to do less of anything.

On the fourth day of the second week, they spent an entire afternoon with a group of other kids playing hide-and-seek beneath the huge, thick vines of a banyan tree that grew beside an inlet at Sadie's Bay. Some of the vines hung straight down over the water, so each time a seeker closed his eyes and counted, a few of the children would lower themselves into the ocean with their mouths and noses just barely above water. It was a clever hiding spot.

At sunset, just as the game was beginning to break up, a boat pulled into the inlet. Kim, who had been hiding in the water, let out a gasp as its bow appeared between the vines. For a second she was certain it was their Grimstone fishing boat, but as the vessel turned to set anchor she saw that it had wooden panels on its side. So it was not theirs after all. But it had served to remind Kim of their mission. "What are we doing?" she wailed to Kimo, who was nearby. "We're losing focus."

"You're right," he said. "Johnny Trout could have the boat in Fiji by now." Kim and Kimo climbed out of the water and found the others, who reluctantly agreed that if they were going to find the boat, they needed to put more energy into the search.

The next morning they visited five beaches in a couple of hours, and didn't let themselves enjoy a single one. By the afternoon, they had spent so much time in the car that everyone was on edge. Toby was especially worried about how much Goldie was getting sloshed around as the little car bumped along the potholed roads. "It's not good for him," the boy moaned. "Sometimes his fins bump the glass."

The first time he said this Pippa scoffed and told him it was ridiculous. After that, Toby took to pointing out every single time the fish touched the side of the jar. "Look," he would say as they went over a bump. "It just happened. Look…Again… Look…Look…Look…"

"All right already," said Pippa. "We get it. A goldfish doesn't belong in a car. So the next time we see a pond, why don't you let him go?"

"Don't say that!" Toby cried, but he didn't give up miserably pointing out every time that the fish was jostled in his jar. The boy's mood wasn't helped by the fact that Penny was getting better and better at crawling and wanted out. She wailed at the top of her lungs, flailing her arms and legs and shouting her only word, "Mine! Mine! Mine!" (Which meant *Get me out of this car, I want to use my legs!*) She was as unhappy as the goldfish.

The drive that day was made even more irritating by the fact that every time they turned on the radio (to drown out Toby's monologue and Penny's screaming), they seemed to hear the same song. The song was called "Sick with Love" and was written and performed by their terrible mother Tina, the country-and-western singer who was an island favorite. Tina's voice might have sounded beautiful to other islanders, but to the Fitzgerald-Trout children it sounded like the shriek of an iguana landing on a spike. Too often they had heard that voice saying irritating things, like "You don't want worry lines. They're very unattractive." The children, with the exception of Kimo, decided immediately that they hated the song. Kimo said he liked it because he found the lyrics so confusing that trying to figure them out made the drive to the next beach pass more quickly.

Since "Sick with Love" was the number one hit on the island's pop charts, it could not be avoided, and each time they heard the opening refrain, Kimo begged the others to listen to it one more time. "Please, you guys, come on. I need to know what she's saying." They had discussed the lyrics a dozen times and still could not make any sense of them. They had no problem understanding the first part of the chorus: "You broke my heart. You shut me out. You chewed me up and spit me out...." (Like so many of Tina's songs, this one was about heartbreak.) But the next part was impossible to decipher. It sounded like Tina was singing, "Like a bug and a wombat." But what could that mean? Did wombats chew bugs? Did they spit them out? Was there anything about that situation that had to do with being sick? Or with love? Or with a broken heart?

Pippa thought they should ask Mr. Knuckles, and while they were at it they really ought to do as they had said they would and talk to the grocery store clerk about what he had done for them. Kim ignored this suggestion and offered that the lyrics must be "Like a bug gone out of whack." But the others said that didn't make much sense either.

Toby stopped his monologue about Goldie long enough to sing along with his own version: "You chewed me up and spit me out like a buggy hammock." But when Kimo told him there was no such thing as a buggy hammock, he admitted that was probably true.

Kimo said that he thought maybe the song was inspired by *Ham!*, which *was* the island's most popular television show. "You chewed me up and spit me out like a *Ham!* contestant," Kimo sang, but the others all shook their heads. While it was true that sometimes the contestants on *Ham!* ate their sausages too fast and had to spit them out before they choked, it wasn't exactly an image that made you think about heartache. And to sing the song with these lyrics, the word *ham* didn't sound at all like the way Tina sang it.

At some point, somewhere around the twentieth time they'd heard the song, Kim was struck by the inspiration that Tina was singing, "Like a budding romance." But Kimo made the point that the romance in the song wasn't budding. It was over, or at the very least it was sick. After that, Kimo stopped asking to keep the song on, and the lyrics became an unsolved mystery.

The next morning, Pippa and Toby jointly began petitioning the older two to give up the search for the boat. They both wanted to spend the rest of the summer camping at Pea Tree Beach and promised they wouldn't complain about brizzill bugs or sleeping in the car when it rained. But Kim wouldn't hear of giving up the search. Her reasons were practical. She knew it was raining almost every night, and she had begun to worry that Pippa and Toby, who were both short for their ages, weren't growing properly because of sleeping upright in the car. She didn't have evidence for this theory, but she felt she knew it in her bones. She had put *Find the boat* at the top of her (mental) to-do list and she would not give up.

Kimo agreed with Kim that they should keep driving, though his reasons were not so practical. He was motivated by his hurt and resentment of Johnny Trout, who had not only kicked them out of the cabin they had called home but had also stolen their boat. Kimo wanted to punish his father for all the bad things he had done, but he didn't admit that. Instead he said, "I know it's summer and we should be hanging out at the beach, but the boat's important, and if something's important you have to be willing to make a sacrifice."

Pippa flared up, suddenly furious. "Did you just quote a grown-up to us?"

"No," said Kimo defensively. "What do you mean?"

"I mean, that sounded an awful lot like what that scientist said the night we gave her a ride."

"She wasn't a scientist," said Toby.

"Not that again," snarked Kim, steering to avoid a pothole.

But Kimo was focused on Pippa. "Maybe she did say it. Just because a grown-up says something doesn't mean it's completely wrong."

"Comb your hair, wash your face, brush your teeth," Pippa intoned in a mocking voice. "Grown-ups are so full of wisdom."

"You listen to the things Mr. Knuckles says," Kimo pointed out.

"That's because he doesn't sound like other grown-ups," said Pippa. "And that's another thing we should be doing. We should be going to talk to that grocery clerk. We told Mr. Knuckles we would help him win her back."

Inspired by the reminder of Mr. Knuckles's

heartbreak, Toby began to sing, "You broke my heart. You shut me out. You chewed me up and spit me out...."

"No, no, no," wailed Kim, "not that song again!"

And that was when Toby and Pippa realized that the best way out of the car was not to argue with Kim and Kimo, but to make the car so completely irritating that the older two would give up on the search for the boat.

So it was that a few days later, as they rounded the bend at Skoot's Point, Penny was wailing and flailing in her car seat, Toby and Pippa were crooning at top volume, Kimo was covering his ears, and Kim was so distracted she didn't notice that the car in front of them had stopped in the middle of the road. They were on a collision course with its bumper.

"Watch out!" Pippa screamed, seeing what was coming and breaking out of the song. Instinctively Toby clutched Goldie to his chest. Kimo gripped his seat just as Kim jolted to her senses, hit the little green car's brakes, and skidded them to a stop inches away from the bumper.

They all sat for a second in shock, their hearts racing with relief at the nearness of the near miss.

Kimo was the first to speak. "What's going on?" He had noticed that not only were the cars in front of them stopped completely but people had turned off their engines and were getting out of the cars to walk up the shoulder of the road that ran beside the ocean. They were going to look at something farther up ahead. But what?

The Fitzgerald-Trouts were too curious not to find out. They clambered out of the car and began picking their way along the gravel shoulder of the road. Even with feet as tough as theirs, it was hard walking on that gravel. Kim found herself picturing the closet full of shoes. If only I had those tap shoes, she thought, *tap, tap, tap, tippity, tap…*

As they walked farther, they could see clouds of billowing smoke rising up from the road ahead. "You think it's a fire?" asked Kimo.

"Or an accident, maybe," said Kim. "Could be the smoke is from the engine."

"I don't want to see an accident," said Toby.

"I don't want Penny to see one either," added Pippa.

A boy walking past them toward his car must have overheard because he called out to them, "It's no accident."

"What is it?" asked Kimo.

"Only the coolest thing I've ever seen," said the boy, flashing a wild grin of excitement at the Fitzgerald-Trouts before they lost sight of him in the crowd.

"Let's go," Kimo said, and picked up his pace and pushed through the crowd that had come to a standstill. People were pulling out cameras, holding them up over their heads, trying to get photographs of whatever it was that was causing the smoke. The children pushed on, saying, "Excuse me, excuse me"—polite but determined.

At last, when they broke through, they found

something so unexpected that it was worth the struggle. A long red-and-black river of swollen lava had come down from the volcano at the top of the mountain. Having scorched a path through the forest, it was now pouring its burning mass across the road, making it impassable.

Far away, on the other side of the seething river of molten rock, which looked almost puffy with heat, they could see a crowd gathered, composed of people who had been driving their cars in the other direction. Between the two crowds swelled the mass of roiling stone that was so hot, in places flames leapt from it like bright red party streamers.

But what was causing the smoke?

They looked to the right at the giant cloud. Now they saw that it was above the ocean. So once the lava poured across the road and over the gravel shoulder, it fell down the side of the cliff and dropped into the water. But why smoke? Was the ocean on fire?

They made their way to the metal safety bars

meant to stop cars and people from careening over the edge of the cliff, and they peered down at the fiery rock dripping over the cliff into the sea. As each drop of liquid stone hit the ocean, it brought the water around it to a boil. This boiling water was creating the huge plume of what looked like smoke but was really steam. "He's right," said Toby. "This is only the coolest thing I've ever seen." But Kim and Kimo were thinking just the opposite. They were thinking that the volcano waking up was another sign that things on the island were not right. The island was sick and it was throwing up, just like Pippa had thrown up when she'd had the flu. But what in the world makes an island sick?

Kimo reached his hand out to test the heat coming off the lava. Even though it was a few feet away, he felt it on his palm like a scorch from a hot stove. "Unbelievable," he said as he quickly pulled his hand back.

"Mount Muldoon erupted," said Pippa. "I thought it was dormant."

"It's woken up," said Kim, "just like that scientist said." She glared at Toby before he could say that the woman wasn't a scientist. Toby shrugged and looked away. He had very particular ideas about the woman's identity, but he kept them to himself as they started back to the car, climbed in, and made a U-turn out of the traffic, heading down the coastal road in the other direction.

After two weeks spent visiting every single place on their boat launch list, the Fitzgerald-Trouts were still no closer to owning the Grimstone fishing boat than they had been when Kimo's name had first been drawn. In fact, they were further away. The boat—with its fishing poles, captain's chair, silver wheel, and ladder down to the cabin that had a table, two bunks, a kitchen, and a bathroom—seemed to have vanished.

In silence, they drove back to their campsite

at Pea Tree Beach and began to make lunch. They were surprised to discover that there were almost no groceries in the car—only a couple of tubes of crackers and a can of spaghetti that Kimo fished out from under one of the seats.

We have to get groceries today, Kim thought, and then it occurred to her, with a heavy heart, that she would have to change the number one thing on her (mental) to-do list from *Find the boat* back to *Find a house*. Just the thought of this task overwhelmed her. She kept trying to get herself to say the words—*I can, I can, I can*—but she couldn't, she couldn't, she couldn't. Finding a house seemed more impossible than ever.

Kim wasn't the only one who was unhappy; even Pippa and Toby, who had agitated to stop the search for the boat, were now realizing how much they had begun to believe the boat would eventually be theirs. Every night since the North Shore Summer Fair, they had fallen asleep imagining that they would soon fall asleep in one of those little bunks. Every morning they had made breakfast, imagining cooking in that little kitchen. Now here they were at Pea Tree Beach once again, scraping together the coals of their old campfire and digging through the bushes for dry firewood so that they could start a fire to keep the brizzill bugs away.

A cloud settled over the Fitzgerald-Trouts as they took turns stirring the pot of spaghetti and watching Penny, who was dragging her octopus around in the sand.

To make herself feel better, Kim tried to think of the things on her list that she *could* cross off.

Find a house
Get groceries (also
    brizzill bug spray,
    new notebook)
Teach Toby geography
Clean baby seat
Cut Toby's hair

Fix flashlight
Repair engine??
Return library books

"Toby, please name the continents," said Kim.

"France," said Toby. "Beijing. Ohio. Winnipeg. Kenya…"

"Those aren't continents," Pippa snarled.

"Yes they are," said Toby, yanking at Pippa's hair.

"Ouch!" Pippa yelped, naming the continents— "Asia, Africa, Europe, North America, South America, Australia, Oceania…"

"Oceania's not officially a continent," corrected Kimo. "It's a group of islands in the Pacific." But Pippa wasn't listening; she was struggling to get away from Toby. When she couldn't, she grabbed for Toby's hair, which was so long that she could pull it.

"I need a haircut," Toby wailed to Kim.

"I know," said Kim, "it's on my list."

"Is Mr. Knuckles on your list?" asked Pippa.

"Why should he be?" said Kim.

"We never went to see that grocery clerk, Asha. We were going to tell her how he helped us," pointed out Pippa. "We promised him we would."

"His heart got chewed up and spit out like a bug and a wombat." Kimo tried for a joke but no one was in the mood.

"Fine," said Kim. "We have to get groceries anyway."

Pippa and Kimo found Asha in the enormous warehouse at the back of the grocery store, standing at a counter over a big metal bowl of macaroni noodles. She was ladling mayonnaise out of a tub the size of a fishing buoy and mixing it into the noodles with her gloved hands. "We're looking for someone named Asha," Pippa said.

"I'm Asha," the woman answered with a friendly smile. "You here about the picnic? Forty ham sandwiches and ten gallons of macaroni salad coming right up." She wore a white chef's coat, and her red hair was pulled up into a ponytail. "Hope you don't mind waiting a couple of minutes. I'm just finishing it now."

"We're not here about the picnic," Pippa began. "We're here about Mr. Knuckles."

"Hurley?" Asha asked. Her hands, in the macaroni, stopped moving.

Pippa was thrown off by the use of Mr. Knuckles's first name. She hadn't known it before and it made her falter. "Hold on a second," she said, trying to collect her thoughts. How should she best tell the story of Mr. Knuckles—Hurley—and his attempt to help them? How could she make it sound heroic?

While she thought, Kimo grinned at Asha and said, "This place is amazing." He was surveying the warehouse where all the grocery store's food preparation happened. There was a huge bakery area where a woman (also in a white coat but wearing a chef's hat) stood over a doughnut machine that was dropping raw dough into boiling oil; a man nearby was writing *Happy Birthday, Bunny* in blue frosting on a cake. In the deli section, a butcher wearing a shower cap was cutting a huge hunk of pink meat on an enormous silver slicing machine. In the fish section, a woman in black rubber overalls was pulling live lobsters from buckets and putting them in a big, clear plastic tank. At the far corner of the room, in the garden section, a florist was trimming the stems of roses, making bouquets.

"I've never seen anything like it," Kimo said, then he noticed that he was shivering. "Why's it so cold?" He wrapped his hands around his arms and rubbed them to keep warm.

"We open and close the doors"—Asha pointed to a tall row of silver freezers that lined the wall closest to them—"to stock the store with frozen stuff. It cools things down."

Then she added, "I like it. It reminds me of my childhood."

"Where did you grow up?" Kimo couldn't help but ask.

"The far north," said Asha. "And no, I didn't own a pet reindeer, but I did do a lot of ice fishing." She laughed as she said this, a warm, happy laugh like waves sloshing over pebbles. "I only say that because when people hear I'm from the north they always ask about reindeer, and they never imagine I lived near the beach."

"I know what you mean," said Kimo. "People here, island visitors, are always asking me if I've swum with a dolphin." He had decided he liked talking to Asha. "What's ice fishing?"

"You cut a hole in the ice and drop a fishing line down."

"Cool," said Kimo, then he laughed at his own joke. Ice fishing wasn't just cool, it was *cold*.

"Is that why your heart is as cold as a frozen steak?" piped up Pippa, who had been listening and was remembering that part of Mr. Knuckles's story. Asha looked as if she had been slapped, and Pippa immediately regretted what she'd said.

"My heart isn't cold," Asha said. "It's the furthest thing from cold. I'm happy for Hurley. I really am." But Asha didn't sound happy; she sounded like someone trying to be happy, and Pippa saw that her lips were quivering the way Penny's did right before she cried. Asha sighed and said, "Hurley is a special man. And she's a lucky lady."

"Who is?" asked Pippa.

"I don't know," said Asha. "I don't know anything about her." Pippa was confused. What lucky lady? Mr. Knuckles didn't have a lady. She saw that Asha had begun stirring the macaroni frantically, as if a well-mixed salad might take her away from the conversation.

"We're friends of Mr. Knuckles, that's all...." Pippa urgently wanted to explain. "We came to tell you something nice he did for us. How he tried to help us claim a fishing boat that Kimo won at the

North Shore Summer Fair. He's a very nice man! We thought if we told you what he did, you might feel differently. It really isn't his fault that Johnny Trout had already claimed the boat and taken it away."

"I don't think I can talk about this," Asha said, blotting at one eye with the back of a gloved hand. With the other, she picked up a saltshaker and loosed salt over the macaroni, then changed the subject. "Did you say that Johnny Trout has a boat?"

"Yeah," said Kimo. "Why? Do you know him?"

"No," said Asha, relieved to be discussing something else, "but I thought maybe that meant there was another shipment coming in, and I should tell the garden section to expect a big order of Blue Miracle Sunshine Food."

Pippa and Kimo blinked at each other. They had no idea what the woman was talking about.

"Blue M-M-Miracle Sunshine Food?" stuttered Kimo. "Does Johnny usually order it?"

"He did the last time he had a shipment," said Asha. "A few weeks ago."

"Shipment of what?" asked Pippa.

"I don't know," said Asha, then she added, "Actually, if I remember right, it was Professor Mumby who called and placed the order. She said that she and Johnny needed three hundred jugs of the stuff. When I asked what it was for, she told me to mind my own business."

"Sounds fishy," said Pippa.

"Who's this Professor Mumby?" asked Kimo, thinking the name sounded familiar.

"Beats me," said Asha.

But Kimo was realizing that he didn't have to ask; he already knew. He reached into his pocket and felt the edges of the business card he had collected at the fair. The card said: BUG TROUBLES? CALL PROFESSOR MUMBY. He clenched the card in his hand, and an idea began to take shape in his mind.

Bug Troubles?
call Professor Mumby
555-8641

The five siblings stood next to their grocery cart in the middle of the produce section—between pyramids of oranges, mangoes, muskmelons, lychees, and coconuts—discussing the plan. Kimo had quickly caught Kim and Toby up on their conversation with Asha, explaining that they now knew his father was using the boat to bring shipments of something onto the island, something that needed vast quantities of Blue Miracle Sunshine Food, whatever that was. He showed them the business card. "The stuff they're bringing on the boat, it's helping people who have bug troubles."

"Johnny Trout is *helping* people?" Pippa sounded skeptical. "You know what I think?" They all looked at her blankly. They didn't know what she thought. "I think he's doing something *illegal*."

"Why?"

"When Asha asked what it was for, they told her to mind her own business."

Kim nodded. "Johnny Trout doing something illegal makes sense. I mean, our parents are, by definition, terrible."

"One of them is already in jail," Toby offered.

"And Tina and Clive *should* be in jail," Pippa added, "for abandoning a baby." They all looked down at Penny, who was the baby in question. She was sitting on the floor of the grocery store, eating a banana, and when she saw all their eyes on her at once, she raised the banana in her fist and shouted, "Mine!"

"Someone teach her a new word," said Kim.

"Another thing to put on your to-do list," said Pippa.

Kimo was looking down at the business card again. BUG TROUBLES? CALL PROFESSOR MUMBY. "The first thing we should do is just what the card says. We should dial the phone number and say we have bug troubles."

"Then what?" asked Kim.

"Then we fish around for information and find out what this Professor Mumby lady knows about Johnny Trout and the boat."

"We have to be sly," said Pippa. "If it's illegal, she's not going to tell us very much."

"I can be sly," said Kimo, who wasn't entirely sure he could be sly, but wanted to try it. Anything to get their boat back. "Before we do another thing, we need to find a pho—"

But Kimo wasn't able to finish his sentence because just at that moment, the floor beneath their feet began to shake and the ceiling above their heads began to shimmy and the walls around them began to rattle and the pyramids of fruit began to tumble.

"*Knockabout!*" the children all shouted.

Kim bent down and scooped up the baby and they all started toward the exit as fruit cascaded into the air. An avalanche of oranges, mangoes, coconuts, muskmelons, and lychees collapsed around them. They had gotten only a few feet when they found themselves trapped; their arms and legs churned, their bodies slid. Trying to move forward was like trying to run inside a pile of giant, soft marbles. The Fitzgerald-Trouts could not get anywhere.

Toby was holding Goldie in his jar and doing everything he could to keep the fish upright as he himself slipped frantically in the sea of brightly colored fruit. "Help," he shouted as he and the goldfish were buried in oranges, "help!" He was afraid the jar would tip to its side and the water would come pouring out the holes in the top. "Help!"

Then, as suddenly as it had started, the knock-about stopped. The fruit stood still. Trapped inside the mound of oranges, Toby slowly raised Goldie's jar so that he could peer into it. Goldie stared at Toby. He looked unharmed but surprised to suddenly be surrounded by a world so exactly the same color that he was.

Toby poked his head up out of the pile of oranges and looked for his brother and sisters. He could see their arms and legs sticking out of other mounds of fruit. Then one of the mounds spoke. "Everyone okay?" It was Kim, buried in muskmelons.

"Yes," they all answered. Slowly, they each pushed aside the produce and found footing on the floor. They shrugged off the fruit and got to their feet, leaving behind their grocery cart and moving toward one another, checking in: "You okay?"

"Yeah, you?"

"Yeah, you?"

Before they knew it they were in one big,

ten-armed hug that from the outside must have looked like a football huddle. They held on to one another tightly for a few seconds, and then, when they were sure they were all fine, Kimo took a step back and finished the sentence that he'd begun just as the knockabout started: "We need to find a phone."

"Let's talk to Mr. Knuckles," offered Pippa. She secretly wanted the chance to check on the heartbroken man.

A minute later they were crowded at the top of the metal stairs knocking on Mr. Knuckles's door for the second time in as many weeks. It took him a while, but Mr. Knuckles did, at last, swing the door open, and just like the time before he looked as if he'd climbed off the couch to greet them. "Fitzgerald-Trouts," he said without enthusiasm, then he let the door hang open behind him as he started back down the dark hall.

"Wait," said Pippa, taking his arm and steering

him toward the apartment's kitchen. "You need to get up. You've got to stop feeling sad about Asha."

At the sound of the name Mr. Knuckles seemed to crumple.

Pippa propped him up and said, "Please, Mr. Knuckles, I don't know what happened between the two of you, but she seems to still like you. She said she's happy for you. She said you're a special man."

"Then why she go date with other guy?"

"I don't know." Pippa shook her head. "I don't get it. Maybe you should talk to her. Maybe there's been a misunderstanding." Mr. Knuckles looked confused. "Like a mistake," Pippa explained.

"But she go date. How I make mistake?"

"I don't know," said Pippa again. "Maybe she made the mistake."

"Then she come to me," said Mr. Knuckles, shaking his head. It occurred to Pippa that Mr. Knuckles was so humiliated by Asha's rejection of him that he didn't want to talk to her again. This made about as much sense to Pippa as a bug and a wombat or a buggy hammock, for that matter. She looked to Kim for clarity.

"Come on, Mr. Knuckles," Kim chimed in, "let us make you a cup of tea." Kim opened the cupboard to look for the box of tea bags that Kimo and Toby had bought a couple weeks before.

"Mr. Knuckles," said Kimo, "can I use your phone?"

Mr. Knuckles nodded and gestured toward an old-fashioned punch-button phone that hung from the wall. Then he sighed miserably and said, "I go sleep." He turned back toward the hallway.

"Fine," said Kim, who thought it better that the man not hear Kimo's conversation. "We'll bring you a cup of tea." She grabbed the kettle and began to fill it at the sink, noticing that Toby had found a pair of bongo drums and was sitting on the floor of the kitchen playing with them. For the millionth time, Kim asked herself how her little brother always managed to do the absolutely most irritating thing possible in any given situation. "Stop that," Kim said to Toby. "Kimo needs to make a phone call." Toby frowned and ignored her, tapping on the drums with the tips of his fingers while Kimo punched the phone number from the business card into the telephone.

The phone rang a few times, and then a woman answered. "Hello?"

"Is this Professor Mumby?" Kimo asked. In an effort to be sly, he was talking with the phony British accent that he had used to sound like the police inspector from *The Nosy Ninja*.

"Yes," said the professor. "Who's this?"

"Someone with bug trouble, m'lady," Kimo replied. The accent sounded ridiculous, and Pippa and Kim—who were pressed close to him, trying to listen—cringed, thinking the professor would surely catch on to the fact that she was talking to an impostor, and worse, an eleven-year-old one.

But the professor didn't catch on, or if she did, she didn't care. "You've called the right place, *mon ami.*" The professor replied as if she were French. So she probably knew Kimo was an impostor, and it didn't matter to her. Maybe she was used to people calling and pretending to be someone else. Whatever the professor and Johnny were up to, it *must* be illegal.

"Very good," said Kimo, then added, "I hear Johnny Trout's got another shipment coming in."

"That's right," said the professor. "I just heard about the shipment myself."

"So what's in it that's going to stop the bugs?" Kimo was fishing for information.

There was silence on the other end of the line. For a moment Kimo thought he had scared the professor off. Then the woman spoke again. "Whamack," she said, "guaranteed to stop brizzill bugs."

Kimo frowned. "Whamack? What's whamack?"

"Whamack's a plant," the professor answered.

"Ahh!" said Kimo, forgetting to be sly. "I bet you feed it Blue Miracle Sunshine Food, don't you?" Kimo was putting the pieces together.

"We feed it other things too," said the professor with a sinister laugh, then her voice suddenly turned threatening. "Why all the questions?"

"Just curious, m'lady," Kimo quickly recovered. "I want to know what I'll be buying."

"Fine," said the professor, "how many plants do you want?"

"How much are they?"

"A thousand dollars each," said the professor.

The number was so enormous that Kimo almost dropped the phone. He looked at Kim and Pippa, who were both shaking their heads. They were never going to be able to get ahold of a thousand dollars. Kimo put his hand over the phone and whispered to them, "We have to bluff. We can't give up now." The girls both nodded.

The professor must have sensed Kimo's

hesitation and taken it for some form of bargaining, because now she said, "Worth every penny. We've never had a complaint. Ask around."

"I believe you," said Kimo coolly, "but one plant is enough."

"Fine," said the professor. "They'll be arriving tonight. Cross-Eyed Cove. Five o'clock." Kimo looked at the clock on the kitchen wall and saw that it was almost two-thirty. So they had two and a half hours until the meeting. "I'll be there," he said.

Suddenly the professor added, "Cash only."

"Of course," said Kimo, who had no intention of showing up with any money anyway.

"And no cops," added the professor ominously. "You got that?"

"Yes, m'lady," said Kimo, who now knew for certain that the professor was no lady; she was most certainly a criminal.

"Any sign of cops and you won't get the delivery," she added. "You won't even know we were there."

"Got it," said Kimo, then he hastily added, "Cheers." It was the way he thought British people said good-bye.

"*Au revoir*," said Professor Mumby with a laugh.

As Kimo hung up the phone, he noticed his jaw was clenched with tension. As much as he wanted to find the stolen boat, he didn't feel entirely comfortable plotting to do something illegal, so when a loud whistling filled the kitchen he almost jumped out of his skin. He thought it must be the police coming to arrest him, but it was only the kettle coming to a boil.

Kim lifted it off the stove and began to make the tea as Kimo filled the girls in on the parts of the conversation they had missed. They all agreed that Kimo had been right to say he was bringing the money, otherwise the professor would not have set up the meeting. And they agreed that they couldn't call the police or, as the professor had threatened, Johnny might disappear with the boat before they even knew he was there.

"We can't get money. We can't call the police.

What can we do?" Kim asked, eager to prepare in some way for this terrible meeting with their terrible parent.

"We can find out what a whamack is," said Kimo matter-of-factly. "We can figure out why it's illegal."

"Whamack," said Toby, looking up from the bongo drums for the first time. "But of course…" He was pretending to understand because he thought this was another thing—like geography—that he was supposed to know.

"What is it?" asked Kim. "None of us have ever heard of it."

"Oh," said Toby, dropping the charade, "I dunno what it is either." He turned his attention back to the bongos.

"We should definitely find out," said Kim. "These are real criminals we're dealing with. It would be good to know what we're walking into."

Pippa shrugged and said, "I know where we can find out."

"Where?" asked Kimo.

"Moon Ear Tation," Pippa said, remembering that sign in Helvetica font that had been eaten by jabberwills.

"Of course." Kim smiled. "That plant scientist will know all about them."

CHAPTER
13

They stood in the parking lot outside the laundromat eating a quick lunch of crackers and cheese. Because of the knockabout they'd never gotten their groceries, so Kim went back inside to do that while the others changed Penny's diaper and loaded themselves into the little green car. When groceries were packed into the trunk (with the milk and other perishables in the cooler that was stocked with ice), they drove off, excited to be on the trail of the boat once again.

Twenty minutes later, as Kim turned down the road between the maha trees that led to the research station, they heard a peculiar buzzing noise. The noise seemed to get louder and louder the closer they got to the station. Kimo thought the noise might be brizzill bugs (the bugs had gotten even more plentiful in the days since the flood), but as they turned the corner and came into the dirt clearing in front of the research building, they saw that the noise came from a small helicopter—the size of a coconut—hovering in the air. Kim parked the car and they climbed out, staring up at the helicopter that was only a few feet above them.

Penny seemed to have some affinity for the helicopter. She was reaching her pudgy arms up into the air, pleading, "Mine, mine, mine." But the helicopter did not come to her; instead it buzzed off toward a long row of greenhouses. Penny called out to it again, and when it did not reappear she began to cry.

Pippa scooped the baby up. "Shh," she said, "it's okay."

"Mine! Mine! Mine!" The baby was sobbing and heaving herself from side to side, trying to get out of Pippa's arms, as if that would somehow get her closer to the vanished copter.

"I'll find her octopus," Kimo said, heading for the car. Just then the front door of the research station banged open and a woman came barreling down the steps, shouting, "Watch your baby!"

"She's fine," Kim said defensively.

The woman, who had a long mane of pale hair, turned her fury on Pippa. "You can't let her get close to a copter like that! Do you know what could have happened?"

"She wasn't anywhere near the copter." Pippa was indignant. "And we would never let her get hurt."

"It's not her I'm worried about," said the woman. She was wearing yellow pants and a yellow jacket that revealed a white shirt. Pippa couldn't help thinking that she looked like a half-peeled banana. "Do you know how many years of research went into building that device? Do you know how much it cost?"

The children blinked with surprise. Was she really more worried about the copter than the baby?

"It's got a camera fastened to its belly," the woman continued. "That copter is the only known way to get close enough to a volcano to study it without getting burned."

"No it's not," said Kimo. "You can use a lava suit."

The woman adjusted the lapels of her yellow jacket and said, "What are you talking about?"

"Lava suit," said Kimo, looking to his brother and sisters for confirmation. "It's bright and metallic and kind of soft-looking. Like an oven mitt turned inside out, only with eyeholes cut in it."

"Never seen one, never heard of one," said the woman, patting down her hair. She was constantly adjusting herself.

"But Leaf has one," said Kim.

"Leaf who?" the woman said with a shrug. Now the Fitzgerald-Trouts were confused. They looked at one another, then they looked around. They were in the grassy clearing surrounded by maha trees. They could see the research building and in front of it the sign for MOON EAR TATION. This was precisely the spot where they'd dropped off the scientist who called herself Leaf. She had told them about the letters of the sign and the jabberwills with big teeth that came out at night to eat them.

"She's the plant scientist," Kim said. "She works here. She studies plants that grow on the edges of the volcanoes. We've come to talk to her."

The woman picked at a tooth with a long fingernail. "There's never been anyone here by that name, and I've been here twenty years." She tugged on her jacket, straightening it. "If that's why you're here, you'd better go. This is a research facility. Private property." She turned and started back up the steps.

"Wait," said Kim. "We met Leaf the other night and we dropped her off here. All five of us did. Six, if you count Toby's goldfish."

The woman shrugged again. "You sure you didn't make this story up? The kind of suit you just described wouldn't work in a volcano. It would conduct heat, not stop it."

"Yes!" Pippa raised her fist in the air. "That's exactly what I said after we met Leaf. I knew it wasn't a proper invention. Remember, Kimo? That's what I said."

"She did. She said exactly that." Kimo smiled at Pippa, realizing that his little sister had a knack for invention.

"So what?" the woman snapped. "I've gotta get back to work. I'm not a babysitter." She yanked open the door of the research building and headed in, letting the screen door slam shut behind her.

They drove back along the road to town in uneasy silence. They had come to the research station to ask a question about whamack plants, but instead of having their question answered they had stumbled upon another question. Now they had two things they needed to know: What were whamack plants? And who was the woman in the lava suit?

"Actually we have three questions," Pippa declared from the backseat. "What was the thing she was wearing, since it definitely wouldn't stop lava from hurting whoever was wearing it."

"That's not an important question," Kim countered, looking at Kimo, who nodded in agreement.

"It's important to *me*," said Pippa, and suddenly all the frustration she had experienced while they'd driven around the island listening to Tina's song came back to her. "Just because you two are the oldest and sit in the front seats doesn't mean you always get to decide everything. Toby and Penny and I get a vote too. Right, Toby?"

"Yeah!" said Toby. He loved when Pippa's temper was used to help his own cause and not directed at him, as it so often was.

"Right, Penny?" Pippa turned to ask the baby, who chose that moment to spit out a puddle of milk. Pippa mopped up the milk, then glared at Kim and Kimo. Her temper had come to a boil. "Turn off the car."

"We have only an hour before the meeting with Professor Mumby and Johnny Trout, but if you want to spend it on the side of the road arguing, that's fine, just fine." Kim pulled over and turned off the engine.

They sat in grumpy silence for a moment, watching through the windows as a single silver cloud floated over them. Then Pippa spoke. "I would just like to take a minute to try to understand what happened the other night back there in that clearing."

"Fine," said Kim. But she didn't sound fine.

"We all definitely met Leaf," said Pippa. "We wouldn't have known about the research station if she hadn't shown it to us. So why hasn't that lady heard of her?"

"Maybe Leaf doesn't really work there," said Kimo. "Maybe she's someone who pretends to work there."

"Why would she do that?"

"We have no idea," said Kim. "That's the point. It doesn't really make sense."

"Or it was a dream," said Kimo. "What if the knockabout made us hit our heads and have a crazy dream?"

"All of us? Together at the same time? Hitting our heads and dreaming the same dream?" Kim was more than skeptical.

"We saw her before the knockabout," said Pippa. "On the road with the ax. That was before the knockabout."

Toby had been sitting in silence, but finally he couldn't take the pointless debating for another second. He had to try to explain himself. "She wasn't a scientist," he said firmly.

"Please, Toby," Kim said with a groan. "No aliens."

"He can say whatever he wants," said Pippa.

"She wasn't an alien," Toby said. "She was Maha."

"That's right," Pippa said. "We were in the clearing, surrounded by maha trees." She had no idea what Toby meant, but she had fought so that he could be heard and she was not going to let him go unheard.

"Not maha the tree," Toby patiently explained, "the other maha…"

"What other maha? Is this something from Tobyworld?" Pippa asked.

"No," said Toby, "this is from our world. I'm talking about Maha the goddess." Kim gave another groan, but Toby continued. "We learned about her in school…." He was remembering a legend his kindergarten teacher had told the class, about a goddess who lived in the forests on Mount Muldoon and whose name was Maha.

"I remember that legend," said Pippa, "and you know what? They say Maha always appears at night, on a road, in disguise."

"The lava suit," said Kimo. "That was a disguise. And remember how she disappeared? They say Maha always disappears as quickly as she appears." Kimo had learned the legend when he was in kindergarten too. "Toby, you're brilliant." To Kimo it was as if Toby's words had descended from the sky, carried on that brightly lit silver cloud. He absolutely knew that Toby was right.

"Indeed," agreed Pippa, who could see no other explanation for Leaf's appearance and disappearance. "If I were a goddess who lived in a forest, I would call myself Leaf."

But Kim was shaking her head. "You've got to be kidding," she said. "You guys don't actually believe we were visited by a goddess."

"There's no other logical explanation," said Kimo.

"A goddess isn't logical," said Kim.

"Not everything is logical," said Toby, lifting Goldie in his jar and looking into the fish's unblinking eyes.

"You guys go ahead and remember the legend, but you know what I remember?" Kim continued, "I remember the day we were in the flooded house talking about just how many ridiculous stories there are on this island."

"You were talking about it," said Pippa. "I don't remember agreeing."

Kim banged her hands on the steering wheel in frustration. "What does it matter whether or not it was Maha? We now have less than an hour before we're supposed to meet the shipment and we don't have the money we're supposed to have and we don't have any idea what we're walking into.... We need to answer that question before we answer anything else."

"She's right," Kimo said, turning to Pippa and Toby. "What is a whamack plant? Why is it illegal? That's the reason we came here. That's what we've got to figure out now. We don't want to meet Johnny Trout and Professor Mumby without knowing."

"Right," said Kim, turning the key in the ignition.

"Once again you're deciding," said Pippa.

"I'm not deciding," said Kim. "It's obvious." But driven by her need to find them a home, she *was* deciding. She pushed on the gas pedal and the car sputtered off. "We'll be lucky if we make it. The engine sounds terrible."

"Make it where?" asked Pippa. "Where exactly have you decided we're going?"

"The library," Kim said. "That's where we can find out about whamack plants." Kim could see Toby glaring at her in the rearview mirror. "I'll make it up to you guys."

"How?" asked Toby.

"In the trunk, in the cooler, I have a couple cans of Uncle Ozo's." Uncle Ozo's was a bubble-gum-flavored soda that was made in a small factory near the harbor. It was an island delicacy and was mentioned in all the travel brochures and tourist websites about the island.

"You bought Uncle Ozo's?" It was Kimo's turn to be annoyed at Kim. "I gave you that money for groceries." Kimo hated when Kim didn't consult him about purchases.

"Just now when I went back in, the grocery store had a bunch of Uncle Ozo's up by the cash register," Kim explained. "The cans fell and got dented during the knockabout so they were only a penny each."

"That's just like you," said Pippa, "not to ask us if we want dented cans of Uncle Ozo's but to buy them anyway."

"Now you're being ridiculous," said Kim.

"We're not going to be persuaded to go where you want to go just because you give us something sweet," said Pippa.

"I am," said Toby. "Pull over." So Kim again pulled to the side of the road. Toby handed Goldie to Kimo, then got out and ran around and opened the trunk, grabbing two cold cans of Uncle Ozo's. He got back in the car, singing, "Uncle Ozo knows how to cure your woes oh, bubble gum you drink not chew, Uncle Ozo's is fun for you.... Halve your troubles with twice the bubbles." It was the jingle from the TV advertisement. They all knew it because Uncle Ozo's was a proud sponsor of *Ham!* and the advertisement played during every commercial break.

As Kim drove off, Toby cracked open the first can and took a long sip, then he passed the can to the others. Even the baby had a small sip so she wouldn't feel left out. When they'd finished the first can, they opened the second and drank that quickly too. Just as they were finishing that, a loud burp erupted from the backseat. It came from Penny, who followed it up with "Mine."

The others laughed and Pippa patted the baby on the back. "Yes. We know that was yours."

But Kim wasn't laughing. Her eyes were wide with horror. "I've made a terrible mistake," she said. Up ahead she could already see the white stone library surrounded by bright red hibiscus bushes and palm trees. She could feel a bubble of Uncle Ozo's making its way from her belly up through her throat. "What was I thinking buying Uncle Ozo's?" The little green car sputtered toward the parking lot of the library. "I should have remembered that it always makes me... *burp*!"

The children all groaned at once. They understood now what the mistake had been. Uncle Ozo's prided itself on having twice the bubbles, which meant that Uncle Ozo's could be counted on to make them burp. This was usually very fun. They had contests to see who could burp the most or who could burp a line from a song or who could burp the letters of the alphabet. But now was exactly the time when they shouldn't be burping. They needed to go to the library to use the computers to find out on the Internet what a whamack plant was, but at the library burping was absolutely forbidden.

The security guard was very strict. She drove

around the library in her security scooter keeping an eye out for rule-breaking children. When she spotted one, she would descend upon the child, cackling loudly and making a point of nearly running over his or her toes. You couldn't eat or drink or chew gum in the library, and you couldn't talk loudly. You couldn't run or skip or whistle. You couldn't play video games on the library's computers or visit certain banned websites. But most of all, you couldn't burp. The security guard's name was Mrs. Belcher, and she hated burping. She took it very personally, assuming that children who burped were making fun of her because her name, Belcher, was another word for someone who burps. Kim and the others had known children who'd lost their library privileges entirely because they'd burped in front of Mrs. Belcher.

"What are we going to...*burp*...do?" Kim asked, clamping her hand over her mouth.

"We could...*burp*...wait," said Pippa as a bubble emerged from her throat.

"We can't," said Kimo. "We have less than an…*burp*…hour. We need to know why the…*burp*…whamack plant is illegal…so we can…*burp*…prepare…*burp*…." There were four burps in Kimo's statement, which made him realize that only one of them should go into the library. There would be fewer burps that way and fewer chances of the burper being caught by Mrs. Belcher. "Maybe just one of…*burp*…us should go…*burp*…in," he managed to spit out.

Toby was burping so much he couldn't speak, but Pippa managed to ask, "Who?"

"None of us," said Kim, slowing as the car neared the library's parking lot. "We can't…*burp*…go in.…*burp*…We can't." Kim loved the library more than any other place on the island. It had always been a refuge for her. She would go there and take a book off the shelf and dive into another world: a world without terrible parents or broken-down cars or hungry younger siblings. There were huge pillows in piles on the soft carpet in the center of the children's section, and Kim had spent many happy hours lying on those pillows reading about worlds far away from her own. The thought of losing her library privileges was more than Kim could bear.

"Then we have to find out…*burp*…about whamacks…*burp*," said Kimo. "They told us no…*burp*…cops. Why? What is so…*burp*…bad about whamacks…*burp*?"

"There must be another way to find out," said Kim, proud she hadn't burped that time.

But no one could come up with one.

The boat is important, Kim thought. One of us has to make this sacrifice. I am the oldest. I am the one who bought the cans of Uncle Ozo's and let us all drink the doubly bubbly stuff. Kim knew this meant that she was the one who must risk losing her library privileges. "All right," she said to the others, "I'll…*burp*…go."

Slowly she pulled into a parking space. The car's engine was sputtering so badly now that it sounded like it was burping too. She hit the brakes, turned the engine off, and got out of the car without another word (or burp).

The others watched her head across the parking lot and up the ramp that was lined with palm trees. As the huge front doors slid open and Kim entered the library, all of them—even Pippa—were watching her in awe.

CHAPTER
14

As soon as she got inside, Kim spotted the librarian, Mrs. Kinnicutt, crouched down beside a little boy who was clutching a copy of *Stuart Little* and talking in a hushed and serious voice. The book was one of Kim's favorites, and she remembered a day when she too had talked to Mrs. Kinnicutt about it, asking the librarian to explain to her how a mouse could possibly have been born to a human family. She remembered Mrs. Kinnicutt telling her that in a book anything can happen; the usual rules don't apply. That's probably what she's telling the boy right now, thought Kim, and she felt a great longing to go over and join the conversation. But then she looked up and saw the clock on the wall and knew that in her life the rules did apply. She did not have time for anything but whamack.

She headed to one of the computer desks and quietly slid out a chair. She felt a burp rising in her throat, but just as it emerged she pressed the power button on the computer, using the *bing!* sound to cover the noise. It worked. So far, so good.

She clicked on the search engine and was typing the words *whamack plant* when she heard the whir of rubber tires and a low, cackling voice calling out, "Kim Fitzgerald-Trout, where have you been?"

She turned around and saw Mrs. Belcher wheeling toward her, hissing, "Mrs. Kinnicutt tells me you have five overdue library books." Mrs. Belcher had a face like a fish that seemed to be almost folded in half along a line that ran up her nose, a feature that was highlighted by her big, hairy eyebrows. "Five overdue books!"

Kim wanted to say that it wasn't the security guard's job to keep track of overdue books, but she didn't dare open her mouth. Besides, Kim knew that Mrs. Belcher was right. She pictured her (mental) to-do list with the words *Return library books* all the way at the bottom. Why hadn't she remembered to bring those books? They were right out there in the trunk of the car. Now it was too late. Holding her breath, she quickly hit the computer's return button. Up popped a list of websites that had to do with whamack plants. She clicked on the first one just as—"Ouch!"—Mrs. Belcher's rubber tire squashed the toes of her right foot.

"Did you hear me?"

Kim nodded. She was trying to use as few words as possible, since talking seemed to make the burping worse, but she could feel a bubble of Uncle Ozo's rising up from her gut. "Well…where are they?" Kim desperately wanted to explain, but she couldn't talk. So she shrugged instead and said to herself, *I can, I can, I can.*

"Showing disrespect is against library rules," said Mrs. Belcher with a frown that brought together her eyebrows, so they looked like one long insect crawling across her forehead.

"They're in the—" Kim snapped her mouth shut. She wasn't going to let that burp escape.

"The what?" The eyebrow insect quivered furiously.

Kim was running her eyes frantically down the first website entry for whamack plants. A few words stuck out: *carnivorous, Oceania, bugs, mosquitoes, Incata Island.*…She was reading as quickly as she could, racing the burp that was rising in her throat. Up it came as Kim's eyes scanned that website and Mrs. Belcher waited for an answer.

"*Where are they?*" Mrs. Belcher shouted, breaking the library rule.

Kim couldn't stay silent a second longer. "They're in the...*burp!*"

Mrs. Belcher looked shocked. The eyebrow insect divided into two smaller, pointed insects that rose angrily above Mrs. Belcher's eyes. "What was that?"

"Nothing," Kim managed to say through squeezed lips.

"I think you belched," said Mrs. Belcher.

"No, I...*burp!*" Kim slapped both her hands over her mouth.

"Out!" said Mrs. Belcher. "Out right now! And don't come back! Your library privileges are revoked!"

Humiliated and heartsick, Kim leapt from her seat and ran for the doors. "*No running!*" shouted Mrs. Belcher. But Kim had nothing left to lose, so she raced through the doors as fast as she could.

Running across the library parking lot, Kim could hear the noise of burps coming from inside the little green car, and she had the fleeting impression that the car was a large metal frog that wouldn't stop croaking. Then, as she got closer, she saw that it was, in fact, a car, and she began to imagine that an army of frogs was waiting inside; she would open the doors and they would all leap out at her. But when she swung open her door, there were no leaping frogs. Instead she found her four burping siblings sitting in their seats, gripping their swollen bellies. She slid in and slammed the door. "Bad news," she told them.

"What?" they asked, and not a single one of them burped. So maybe the wretched spell cast by Uncle Ozo's was over.

"Whamack plants are carnivorous," Kim said. "That means they eat meat." The running seemed to have gotten rid of most of Kim's burps too.

"There are plants that eat meat?" Kimo shivered, picturing a forest of flesh-eating trees whose branches feasted on dogs, cats, birds—maybe even people. Pippa and Toby were thinking the same thing.

"I used to like the forest," said Toby. Kim saw that he was hugging Goldie protectively.

"The plants don't eat goldfish," Kim explained, "or people. The meat they eat is bugs. A whamack is a bush that has leaves that eat bugs. They grow on an island in Oceania."

"So they have some kind of giant swatter?" Pippa was fascinated, picturing this weird plant invention: a flyswatter growing from a bush, swinging back and forth in the wind.

"No," said Kim, "from what I read, and I could only read a little bit because Mrs. Belcher was there and…*burp*…" Just saying the security guard's name made a bubble erupt from the girl. "An insect lands on the leaf of the plant and the leaf is like a cup with teeth that closes over the insect, and the insect is trapped. It gets dissolved by something that's like stomach acid, something that digests it."

"Why does Johnny Trout have the plants?" Kimo asked.

"I think he must have found them when he was traveling on his boat," Kim said. "He must have sailed to this island in Oceania and figured out that bringing the plants back here was a way to get rich."

That made sense to Kimo, who was thinking about the night his father had locked them out of the house. Johnny Trout had talked about islands without names. Was one of those islands the one with the whamack plants? Once again, Kimo felt hurt and resentment expanding in his chest.

"But why would he get rich?" This was Pippa. "Why are the plants worth so much?"

"They kill bugs," said Toby, who remembered just how awful it had been when he'd been on the roof of the car in a cloud of brizzill bugs.

"So why is that illegal?" Pippa was confused.

Kim shrugged and said, "I saw something on the website—someone brought a bunch of whamacks to a place called Incata Island and something bad happened there, but I didn't have

time to finish reading before Mrs. Belcher…
burp…kicked me out."

"She kicked you out?" Pippa was shocked. It
had always seemed to her that Kim got away with
everything.

"I no longer have library privileges," said Kim,
sitting on her hands to stop them from trembling.
The thought of life without the library was fright-
ening to her.

"Oh, Kim," said Kimo. He knew what an
awful blow this was to his sister.

"It had to be done," said Kim, putting on a
brave face. "Someone had to go in there. We needed
to know what terrible thing we were facing."

"But you didn't find out why the plants are terrible," said Pippa with a hint of accusation in her
voice.

"Maybe the plants aren't terrible," Kim said.
"Maybe it's just Johnny Trout himself."

Kimo nodded; he was picturing his salt-stained
father with the crooked bandanna on his head and

the snarling pig at his heels. "He stole the boat and he took our home away from us. What could be more terrible than that?" It was true, and they all sat in the bald light of this truth for a moment.

Kimo was the first to speak. "We should call the police," he declared. His rage at his father had overcome him.

"Are you crazy?" said Pippa. "If we do, Johnny and the professor won't show up. We'll lose our chance at the boat."

"Johnny's a villain." Kimo clenched his fists. "He might be dangerous."

"The *plants* are dangerous," wailed Toby. "I don't want to go near them!"

"If we want the boat, we've got to risk it." Kim shouted to be heard, because suddenly they were all talking at once, debating what to do next. Even the baby wanted her opinion heard, and began to wail, "Mine! Mine! Mine!"

"No, Penny," Toby quarreled with her, "it's not your boat. It's *our* boat! It belongs to all of us!"

And in the midst of the argument swirling around him, Toby was surprised to discover that he meant this. All his bad feelings about Kimo winning the contest were gone; he found himself willing to face down Johnny Trout and the dangerous plants in order to get the boat back. "Start the car," Toby shouted loudly. "Let's go get our boat before it's too late!"

For once, Kim listened to her little brother. She turned the key, revved the engine, and backed the car out of the parking space.

"Ow bow!" Penny yelped gleefully. "Ow bow, ow bow, ow bow!"

"She has new words!" Pippa's heart swelled with pride.

"Ow boat!" Penny shouted again.

"It's not going to be our boat if we don't figure out what to do next," Kimo said darkly. They all knew he was right. As Kim drove toward Cross-Eyed Cove they began to concoct a plan.

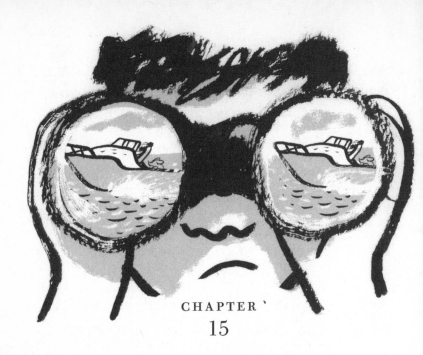

I t was almost five o'clock and the sun was slowly sinking into the ocean, sending waves of pink light out across the water. From his perch in an old concrete bunker on a cliff above Cross-Eyed Cove, Kimo watched with great longing as his shiny, state-of-the-art Grimstone fishing boat headed toward a long concrete wharf. He had the binoculars pressed to his eyes, so his view of the boat was enclosed in a large dark circle. This view, though constricted, allowed him to see the boat in more detail as it motored through the water, tipping this way and that on the pink waves.

"What's happening?" Kim was pacing beside him, squinting with her bare eyes through the long rectangular hole cut in the bunker. Built many years before, the bunker had once been used by the navy to keep track of ships off the island's coast, but now it was abandoned.

"He's talking to someone." Kimo could see Johnny Trout standing at the silver steering wheel; his head, sporting the dirty bandanna, was just barely visible, but Kimo could tell that his father's mouth was moving. "Must be someone down in the cabin," Kimo said, picturing the table, the kitchen, the two bunks, and the bathroom as he had seen them on the photo taped to the side of the boat at the North Shore Summer Fair. That familiar hurt rose up in him as he watched his father, who was now in full possession of the boat that rightly belonged to Kimo and to his brother and sisters.

"Ow boat, ow boat," said Penny, as if she'd been following her brother's thoughts. She was crawling around on the bunker's floor, dragging her octopus across the dirty concrete. The creature had already lost a plastic eye and had a long gash down the seam of one arm.

"I wish he'd hurry up and get here," fretted Kim. "It's going to be dark soon."

"This plan won't work in the dark," Pippa snarled.

Suddenly they heard a shriek as a cloud of lava gulls lifted off the cliff and wheeled through the air around them. The boat was now only a few hundred yards from the wharf, and its arrival had unsettled the birds. One of them flew straight past the bunker, blocking Kimo's view. When the bird had passed, Kimo squinted through the binoculars again. Now he saw something that really hurt: Wendell, the pig, was making his way out from behind the boat's steering wheel. "Johnny must have been talking to the pig," Kimo growled to the others. "I think the pig was sitting at his feet where I couldn't see him."

Kimo watched as Wendell trotted up the boat toward the bow and picked something up with his mouth. It was a rope that lay on the deck of the boat. What was a pig going to do with a rope?

"Look at the wharf," said Kim in a shocked voice. "You're not going to believe who's here." Kimo focused the circles of the binoculars on the wharf, and he saw what the others were seeing. The woman in the yellow suit with the pale hair, the woman they'd met at Moon Ear Tation, was making her way toward the end of the wharf where the boat was about to dock.

"Why is she here?" asked Kimo. "Professor Mumby is the one that's supposed to meet us."

"Maybe she *is* Professor Mumby," said Pippa.

"Her?" asked Kim. "You think she's Mumby?"

"It makes sense. If you're going to import illegal plants, then you need a place to put them. Remember those greenhouses?"

"What's a greenhouse?" asked Toby, who had until that moment been lying under a tree in Toby-world eating marshmallows.

"It's a glass building where they keep…" Pippa started, but her voice trailed off because something very curious was happening below them. Wendell, who had the rope in his mouth, was perched on the railing of the boat.

They all watched with wonder as Johnny swung the boat close to the wharf and the pig leapt off. He landed with a thud on the wharf, then galloped across it to a large metal cleat. Using only his mouth, the pig wrapped the rope around the cleat, thereby fastening the boat to the wharf.

"Wow," said Kim, "he really meant it when he told us he'd trained that pig."

"He said the pig could fetch," added Pippa, "but that was a lot more impressive than just fetching."

"I could've done that," said Kimo, a little lamely.

"Of course you could," said Kim, poking him in the arm, trying to make him feel better because he was still so obviously upset about having been replaced by a pig.

But Pippa shrugged and said, "Who would want to tie up ropes and fetch things for terrible Johnny Trout? Let the pig do it." Kimo smiled at her, feeling a little bit better, then turned his attention back to the action below.

Now that the boat was fastened to the wharf, Johnny was free to leave the steering wheel and so he stepped onto the dock where Professor Mumby was waiting. The two shook hands, and the professor adjusted her lapels and then said something the children couldn't hear. From the way she looked around, it seemed she might be explaining to Johnny that she had talked to someone on the phone who was also coming to meet them.

"She's talking about me,"

said Kimo. "She's saying that I called about the plants and I'm coming to buy one. Boy, I'd like to go down there right now and show my face and make them sorry."

"Which would accomplish exactly nothing," said Kim, looking to Pippa and Toby for backup. "We agreed on a plan and we stick to the plan. The goal here is to get possession of the boat."

"Our plan," said Pippa, "was to wait here and watch and decide how to get the boat once we saw what was happening."

"Yeah," said Kim. "That's what we have to do."

"But our plan has caught up to the present moment," Pippa said. "We're here. We see what's happening. Now we have to do something."

"We need to keep waiting," said Kim, who was chewing her nails nervously and throwing glances down at the boat, the place she hoped they would soon call home. "We don't have money to give them, and we can't just show our faces and talk to them. It'll ruin our chances of getting the boat. Let's see what they do next."

"What if what they do next is drive the boat away?" asked Kimo. "What then?"

"Then we'll lose the boat," said Pippa, making a firm point. "Plus it's getting dark." She gestured to the ocean; the sun had nearly disappeared and the water was now a deep purple. "We need to do something right away."

They heard a loud *bang!* from the wharf below and they all looked down at once. The bang had come from a large cage that Johnny Trout had set down on the concrete. Kimo scrambled, put the binoculars to his eyes, and focused them until he could see what was inside. It was a bushy green-and-purple plant with dozens of leaves that looked like big thorny cups. "Whamack," Kimo said. "They keep them in cages." *Bang!* Johnny set another cage down on the wharf, then stepped back onto the boat. The professor, meanwhile, had gone back to the shore and was driving her truck up the wharf toward Johnny.

So they were going to unload the plants from the boat and load them onto the professor's truck while they waited for the person on the phone. Kimo kept the binoculars trained on the whamack, hoping against hope that one of those meat-eating plants would smell the wretched pig and break out of its cage and attack, consuming Wendell right then and there. It seemed unlikely, but worth hoping for.

"We're really gonna just sit here and watch?" Pippa turned to Kim with a scowl.

"We have to," said Kim, who was now so agitated that she was chewing the skin around her fingernails.

"But this is the part where we swing into action," said Kimo. "This is the part where I tell my father just what I think of him as you guys rush onto the boat and drive it away."

"We can't," said Toby, so suddenly and emphatically that everyone looked at him.

"Why not?" asked Kimo.

"They'd see us coming," said Toby. "Kim's right. We'd have to walk all the way down the wharf to get to the boat and they'd both see us coming." It was true, so obviously true that even Toby, who was usually caught up in his day-dreams, had seen the flaw in Kimo's proposal.

They lapsed into silence and again turned their anxious attention to the scene on the wharf unfolding in the last purple gasp of daylight. Johnny had unloaded a dozen or so plants—each in its large cage—and the professor had loaded these onto the truck. The two were standing near the door to the truck, talking. Johnny glanced at his watch; the professor glanced at hers. Then they looked down the wharf toward the shore and the road. They were looking for the person on the phone who was supposed to meet them. Finally the professor gave a shrug and climbed into the driver's seat of the truck.

"She's given up on the meeting," said Kimo.

"She's gonna drive away. Then Johnny's going to get back on the boat and sail off."

"We're missing our chance," Pippa said, rushing toward the bunker door. But Kim leapt in front of her before the girl could leave. "You can't go down there! We've got to wait," Kim wailed in a desperate voice. She had never allowed herself to sound so completely undone. "I know that's our home and I know he's about to take it away again. But everything in me tells me we have to wait!"

Before Pippa could say a word a surprising thing happened. Johnny walked around the truck to the passenger-side door. He put two fingers in his mouth. Though they couldn't hear it, the children knew that he was whistling to call the pig. They watched as Wendell trotted over. Then Johnny opened the truck's door, Wendell jumped in, and Johnny got in beside his pet. Johnny slammed the door, and the truck—with its load of caged whamack plants—drove off down the wharf, leaving the boat completely unattended.

The Fitzgerald-Trouts looked at one another in disbelief. "Ow boat," said Penny. And she was right. The boat was theirs for the taking.

Driving the boat was surprisingly easy. Just like the car, there was a steering wheel to go left or right and there was a gear with a big F for driving forward and a big R for driving in reverse. Kim quickly figured out that the only thing different was that you didn't press your foot on the gas, you pushed your hand forward on the throttle. Kimo cast the lines off the wharf, then stepped aboard the boat, where the others were already waiting. "All aboard?" Kim shouted into the

moonlight. She had read many books about sea voyages and knew all the lingo.

"Yup," Kimo answered.

Kim shifted the gear to F and turned the silver wheel. *Putt, putt, putt*—the boat slowly peeled away from the wharf. As soon as they were a few yards off, Kim pushed on the throttle. As the engines turned more quickly, the bow of the boat rose up out of the water and they sped forward, trailing a big white wake behind them. Kimo looked at Kim and he didn't even need to say what he was thinking. *You were right to make us wait*, he was thinking. *You did it.* They were taking off in the boat and it now squarely belonged to them. Kimo lifted his palm and Kim high-fived him. Pippa and Toby saw what was happening, and they came over and high-fived Kim too. Kim smiled. "We did it," she said, then she pushed the throttle further, and they sped up, zooming out of the cove and into the open ocean.

The things that were different about driving a boat were wonderful. Kim could either sit in the big captain's chair or stand up in front of it and feel the wind blowing her hair. She could go as fast as she wanted because there were no other boats in sight, or she could stop the boat completely and they could just drift where they were. Add to this the fact that there were no roads, so she could go anywhere, and it was driving like she'd never experienced it: completely carefree. "*Wheeeeeee!*" she screamed in the wind. She thought for a moment that she had never known such freedom or pleasure. She looked around to see if the others were feeling the same thing, and she saw that they were.

Kimo had Penny and the octopus in his arms and he was spinning them, doing a wild jig. Pippa and Toby were racing each other back and forth, up and down the deck until they were so tired they collapsed on a pile of ropes at the bow. With their faces pointed out to sea, they looked like the ship's twin figureheads.

It was amazing to Kim that unlike in a car, her siblings didn't have to be sitting down while she drove. They could move anywhere; they could sleep, eat, cook, read, do jumping jacks. There was room for all of it. Only Goldie didn't quite seem to have a secure spot. His jar was stuck in a cup holder, but it tilted precariously each time the boat sped up.

The sun had set and the moon had risen: a bright fishhook. "Dinner?" Kim called out to Kimo.

"Sounds good," Kimo replied, and he began to prepare one of the fishing rods that sat on the back of the boat. Not much later, he reeled up a large catch, and Kim stopped the boat's engines so that it could drift while they went downstairs to the little wooden cabin.

Once down there, Toby and Penny immediately climbed into the big bunks to try them out. The motion of the drifting boat as it rode up and over the waves caused the children to roll back and forth on the bunks. The baby laughed and grabbed her feet. Imitating her, Toby did the same. Meanwhile Kim began to cook the fish on the stove, and Kimo and Pippa explored the walls of the cabin that were filled with cupboards and drawers. They found a long, wide drawer that held charts showing different parts of the ocean around the island. Pippa unrolled one of the charts on the table and studied it with great interest. She noticed that there were little numbers written all over the part showing the water. Kimo pointed out that the numbers got bigger as they got farther into the ocean, so the numbers must tell how deep the water was. Together they realized that by studying the charts, they could find somewhere that was shallow enough to anchor the boat for that night.

But they didn't know how to use an anchor, so they rifled around until they found the boat's manual. While Pippa was looking it over, Kimo found a large, spiral-bound green notebook with handwriting on the cover and pages of drawings and notes throughout. Wedged between two pages of the notebook was an envelope and on the envelope was written his name. Why *his* name?

He opened the envelope—which was not sealed— and pulled out a piece of very official-looking paper. As he read, a huge grin appeared on his face. When he'd finished he looked up at his siblings. "It's ours," he said, and he waved the piece of paper at them. "It says so right here." The others crowded around and Kimo read aloud the piece of paper that proclaimed Kimo Fitzgerald-Trout the owner of Grimstone Fishing Vessel Serial Number 78d2b.

"It's the deed to the boat," said Kim.

"Indeed," said Pippa, laughing as she realized that the word had never been more apt. "In*deed*."

"We own it." Kimo was shaking his head like he couldn't believe what was happening.

"It's ours," said Toby, pulling baby Penny into a hug.

"No one can take it away from us," said Kim. "No one can say otherwise."

Pippa picked up the green notebook. "What's this?" she asked. On the cover of the notebook were written the words *Research Notes*.

"Who cares?" Kim said. "Let's eat."

But Pippa cared. She was fascinated by the drawings she found in the book, most of which were of plants. After dinner, when they went back up on deck, she brought the notebook, and while her sister and brothers went for a swim, she offered to stay on the boat with the baby so that she could read it by the light of the boat's instrument panel.

All the purple had left the sky, leaving a blackness speckled by stars. The Big Dipper hung like a giant ladle ready to spoon up the ocean. One by one, Kim, Kimo, and Toby jumped off the bow of the boat and into the air, falling through the darkness, then plummeting into the greater darkness of the water. They kicked and splashed and dove under the water, staying close to the still-drifting boat. When they got tired they floated on their backs, staring up at the zoo of stars and naming all the animals they could find: the lion, the goat, the scorpion. Every once in a while they rolled over, took a mouthful of seawater, and spit it into the air like a whale spouting water.

"You can hear them, you know," Kimo said to Kim.

"Hear who?" She hadn't been following his thoughts.

"The whales," said Kimo. "Put one ear underwater and if there's a whale nearby you will hear it singing."

Kim and Toby did as he had suggested, and they heard an astonishing thing: not just one whale calling out with its mysterious, echoing, musical howl but two whales calling back and forth to each other. It sounded to Kim as if two great continents long ago divided by the ocean were speaking across the distance, trying to find a way back to each other. The wonder of this seemed too impossible to communicate so instead, when she lifted her ear from the water, she said simply, "We're swimming with whales."

"I know," said Kimo, caught up in the outlandishness of it all. "We have a house that floats above whales."

"Do they bite?" asked Toby. The older two didn't have a chance to reassure him because Pippa was leaning over the rail of the boat, shouting, "You have to see this!"

"We were wrong," Pippa said as she paced back and forth near the steering wheel of the boat.

The others were sitting, wet on the deck; they had to squint to see one another in the darkness. "Remember how we found out about the whamack plants and Kimo said they must be terrible and Kim said it wasn't the plants that were terrible, it was Johnny who was terrible?" The others nodded their wet heads. "Well, that was wrong," she went on. "The plants *are* terrible." She waved the green notebook. "It's all in here. These are Johnny's notes and clippings about what he's been doing, and what he's been doing is importing illegal, carnivorous plants."

"We already knew that," said Kimo, watching a shooting star burst across the sky.

"But what we didn't know was that the plants are native to some island in Oceania. That's where Johnny found them...."

"An island without a name," said Kimo, remembering his father's description of his travels.

"Sure," said Pippa, "whatever. The plants do fine there, but because they eat bugs they have become very popular on *other* islands. The problem is that on those other islands they cause problems. That's why they're illegal. There was this one island that he mentions in the notebook, Incata Island. Someone brought the plants there to help with a bug infestation and the plants grew into the soil of the island and the roots of the plants caused—"

Kimo interrupted, "Knockabouts, floods, volcanic eruptions…" Suddenly everything they had been seeing on the island made sense to him.

"Yes," said Pippa, "and rain. Lots and lots of rain. Before the people of the island realized what was happening and could get rid of them, the whole island was flooded."

"Remember how we said our island was sick?" Kimo asked Kim.

"I do," said Kim, who had tucked herself up into a little ball with her hands wrapped around her knees.

"Now we know what it's sick with. It's been invaded by killer plants. That flooded house we were in? Soon the whole island will be like that."

Kimo understood now that his father had caused all the island's problems. Of course he had.

Kim hugged her knees tighter. "It doesn't make sense to me," she said, rocking back and forth. "The plants aren't causing the floods. It's the other way around. The floods are causing the bugs and that's why people want to buy the plants."

"It's both," said Pippa, feeling the breeze pick up around them. "Johnny explains that in here too. He says a whamack plant sells itself because it *causes* the exact problem it's supposed to stop. I guess when the plant digests the bugs, they release a gas—"

"They burp?" This was Toby, interrupting.

"Sure," said Pippa. "Call it what you want."

"The gas causes rain somehow," Kimo said, putting it together.

"And the rain causes more bugs," Pippa continued. "You put a new species in a place where it doesn't belong and it can throw everything out of whack."

"People don't know how bad the plants are for the island. And Johnny doesn't tell them." This was Kimo, sounding very bitter. "He just sits back and gets rich. My father is nothing but greedy."

"He's a real villain," said Pippa. They heard several loud splashes, like a pod of whales had slapped the surface of the water.

"Even the whales agree." Kimo wasn't joking.

Toby hadn't said much and had only been following the general outline of the conversation, but now he piped up, "Good thing we have a boat."

"Why?" Kimo asked.

"If there's floods and stuff, we can float." The boy had offered what he could to the conversation and lay back on the deck, looking up at the stars.

"Sure," said Pippa, "but we can't just zoom off into the ocean and leave the island." She was opening the notebook and taking something out to show the others, although it was too dark for them to see it. "Johnny stuck a copy of an article in here that says there have been a few islands where people saw what was happening and were able to stop it. Out of their natural habitat, the plants have a short life span. You have to keep replanting them or they'll die. The people of these islands destroyed the invading whamacks and slowly the islands cured themselves. Volcanoes on those islands erupted and eventually that made the islands bigger and stronger."

"So the volcano erupting isn't bad. The volcano helps the island."

"Yeah," said Pippa, "like when you're sick and you throw up and you feel better."

"Our volcano already erupted once," said Kimo. "Maybe that's a good sign."

"Maybe," said Pippa, "but Johnny and the professor just brought in a brand-new shipment of plants. That can't be good."

The wind was blowing stronger now, and Kimo felt his spirits roused by it. "We have to destroy this load of whamacks," he said. "Then our island might be okay."

"Hey," said Toby, "this is why Maha came."

They all squinted at him. He was lying on his back looking straight up into the darkness as if he might see Maha's face in the pattern of the stars. "Remember the story? She comes when there's trouble. That's what my teacher said."

"*You* were listening to your teacher?" Pippa was surprised.

"I always listen when he says something interesting," Toby solemnly pronounced.

"Leaf—I mean, Maha—said the forests were changing." Kimo suddenly got to his feet. "She said we islanders needed to help." He shook the water out of his hair like a dog. "We've got no choice. We've got to save our island from the whamacks. Who's with me?"

"Me," said Pippa, raising her hand into the wind.

"Me," said Toby, speaking up to the stars. The baby gurgled, so Pippa raised her little fist as if she were voting yes too. Only Kim was quiet. They all looked at her, and they realized that through that entire long, agitated discussion Kim had hardly spoken.

"Don't tell me…" said Kimo, trying to read her thoughts.

Kim shook her head at him emphatically. "We can't go back there," she said. "We've finally got the boat. We've got a home. We worked too hard for this. We can't risk it."

"What are we risking?" Kimo was genuinely baffled.

"All of it," said Kim. "We dock the boat and leave it there, anyone could take it, but most especially Johnny Trout. If we go up there and mess with his plants, he'll try to get back at us. He's got more people to help him than we do. He'll see what's happening and he'll call someone on his cell phone and by the time we get back to the wharf, the boat will be gone."

"You worry too much," said Kimo. "Worry lines are very unattractive."

He was trying to make a joke, but no one laughed, especially not Kim, who suddenly exploded. "I worry too much? I worry too much?" She was saying it over and over furiously, like someone scratching an itch. She leapt to her feet and she shoved Kimo in the shoulders.

He stumbled backward. "Quit it," he said, but she did it again.

"You think I like to worry?" she asked. "Ever since terrible Fitzgerald taught me to drive when I was eight years old, I've been the one who's had to take care of us. I've been the responsible one. I don't like to worry, but I *have* to worry. We won this boat fair and square and I am not going to give up our home just because of some crazy notes in a notebook. They might not even be true...."

"You know they're true," said Kimo.

"I don't care," said Kim. "No one on that island has ever done anything for us." She was looking each of her brothers and sisters in the eye, one by one. They stared back at her, transfixed. They had never heard her talk like this. "Every single thing we have, we have because we earned it. On our own. Why should we go back there now and risk our home to save them?"

"Ow boat," said Penny, who was sitting at Kim's feet. "Ow boat, ow boat."

Kim scooped the baby up. "That's right," she said, "it's our boat."

"This is our boat," said Kimo. "But it's also our island." He looked to Toby and Pippa, who were both nodding in support. "Our whole lives, for as long as we can remember, when we were hungry what did we do? We went to the mountains and we picked fruit from the trees, or we went to the beach and we fished. We caught crabs in the tide pools and picked clams on the reefs. When we needed to keep warm, we cut down branches from the forests and we built a fire. When we needed a place to sleep, we made a bed in the leaves or one in the sand. Maybe you think that no one on that island has ever helped us. But the *island* has helped us. We can't let it drown. It's our home. Remember Maha said if something's important you have to be willing to make a sacrifice."

"She was just another grown-up trying to teach us a lesson," said Kim.

"Maybe," said Kimo, "but she was right. We have to risk the boat if we want to save the island." It was a rousing argument, and Pippa immediately began to clap. She felt absolutely certain that what Kimo was saying was true, plus she felt thrilled to see someone standing up to Kim.

Penny saw Pippa clapping and she started clapping too. "Ow ho," said Penny, smashing her little hands together. "Ow ho, ow ho."

"Yes." Pippa grinned at the baby. "Our home."

"As for driving," said Kimo to Kim, "you don't have to do it all." He stepped over to the captain's chair and sat down in it. Kim blinked in amazement as he turned the key and started the boat's engine.

At that moment Kim could have run over and shoved Kimo out of the captain's chair. She could have insisted on driving. But she didn't, because as she watched him take his place at the wheel it occurred to her that even if she didn't love his plan, she loved him. Kimo, her almost twin. And that meant that for once she should give up her own desire to be in charge and let him take the lead.

As for Kimo, all those years of watching Kim drive must have rubbed off on him. He seemed to know exactly what to do. He stood behind the wheel, pushed the gear to F, and he pressed on the throttle. "We're going to stop my father," he said, like a captain speaking to his crew. "We're going to destroy this shipment of plants. And if you're worried about the boat, don't be." He plucked the deed to the boat from between the pages of the green notebook. "I'll keep this on me," he said, tucking the deed in his back pocket. "That way no one can ever again say that the boat isn't ours." Then he turned the silver wheel and pointed them all back toward the island.

Standing outside the brightly lit greenhouse, the children could see everything that was going on inside. They could see the long row of whamack plants that had been unloaded from their cages and now sat on a wide table. Above the table hung a row of bright, hot sun lamps. They watched as a man dressed all in green stood with his back to them and carefully tended to the plants. The man, who obviously worked for the professor and Johnny Trout, was moving down the row of whamacks, stopping at each bush and breaking off its dead leaves, then gently tamping down its soil and watering it with a blue liquid that he poured from a jug. "Blue Miracle Sunshine Food," Kimo whispered to the others.

On the boat ride to the wharf, they had decided to wait and watch outside the greenhouses for as long as they needed in order to find the right moment to execute their plan to destroy the plants. They knew that once they started there was no turning back. When they'd gotten to the wharf, Kim had gotten off and gone to get the car, which was parked up the hill near the bunker, and Kimo and the others had sailed the boat back out of the harbor to the inlet at Sadie's Bay, where it would be well hidden by the vines of the banyan tree they'd played in. Once they'd tied up the boat, they rejoined Kim, who was waiting for them in the car, parked by the bay.

Kim had offered to drive to the research station on the mountain. She made the excuse that Kimo didn't yet know all the rules for driving a car on the road, but they all knew that it was her way of showing she was on board with Kimo's plan and that she wanted to do what she could to help destroy the whamacks.

Now here they were, looking at those very whamacks, the ones that were so deadly to their island, being lovingly tended by Johnny Trout's henchman. As the man pruned and watered, he sang a tune to himself, and when he got close enough to where the children stood watching on the other side of the glass, they could just barely make out what he was singing. "You broke my heart. You shut me out. You chewed me up and spit me out, like a…" They all pressed their ears closer to the glass but they could not distinguish the words of Tina's mysterious line.

When he had finished trimming and watering all twelve whamacks, the man headed across the greenhouse to a large cabinet filled with equipment, and for the first time the children were able to see his face. Kimo instantly recognized him and felt a flash of fury. He poked Pippa and quietly hissed, "He's the one who gave me the card at the fair. The card that said 'Got Bug Troubles?'"

"So?" said Pippa, wondering what Kimo was so angry about.

"So he must be the guy who heard over the loudspeaker that I had won the boat."

"He was the one who called Johnny Trout?" This was Kim, who had heard their whispering.

"Yup," said Kimo, rocking from side to side, soothing Penny, who slept in the sling across his chest.

"So he's an *evil* henchman," hissed Kim.

Pippa shook her head ruefully and said, "They usually are."

"What's he doing now?" asked Toby. They all turned their attention back to what was going on in the greenhouse.

The man was at the table of whamacks again. He stood at the first bush and lifted the lid on a small jar. Using tweezers, he reached into the jar and pulled something out. Then he dropped the thing into one of the thorny leaf-cups on the whamack. The children watched with astonishment as the cup, sensing the thing, closed around it like a mouth.

"He's feeding the plants," said Kimo.

They watched him do it again, and now that they knew what they were looking for they saw that it was a bug that the man picked out of the jar with the tweezers. They watched the bug struggle helplessly as the leaf-cup closed around it. The plant must have been hungry because the man did this over and over for each of the thorny leaf-cups on the bush. All the while, the man was singing, "You broke my heart, you shut me out, you chewed me up, and spit me out…"

And then for the first time Kimo understood the mysterious line. He turned to the others and said, "You chewed me up, and spit me out, like a bug in a whamack."

"That's it," Pippa said, forgetting to whisper.

"Shh," Kim hissed, tugging them all backward by their sleeves, because Pippa had spoken so loudly that the henchman was walking over toward the windows. The children scrambled farther into the darkness, where they hoped the man—in the brightly lit room—wouldn't be able to see them. He peered out with his face pressed to the glass, and the children held their breath. But he must not have been able to see anything after all, because a moment later he moved away from the glass, back to the table. The children took a deep breath of relief, then Kim whispered, "I guess if Tina's singing about whamacks, she must know about the illegal business."

"She's probably bought a plant or two," said Kimo.

"For all we know, she's an investor," said Pippa. The oldest three children were thinking how it was never a surprise to discover something terrible about their parents. It was one of the few things in life they could really count on.

"But it doesn't make sense," said Toby.

"Sure it does," said Kim. "The thing you need to understand about Tina is that—"

"Not Tina," said Toby, "the song. The plants don't chew the bugs up and spit them out. They chew the bugs up and they swallow them, then they burp." It was a very good observation.

"I guess she's not just a terrible mother," snapped Pippa, "she's a terrible songwriter too." They all suppressed a giggle and were still choking it back a second later when everything went dark. They turned and saw that the lights in the greenhouse had been shut off. They heard a door down at the other end of the greenhouse being opened; Johnny's henchman came out. He glanced around, pulled the door shut, and started off down the grassy path toward the front of the building.

Kim and Kimo exchanged a look, then turned to Pippa and Toby and gestured for them to stay where they were. Quickly Kimo unstrapped Penny from his chest and handed the sleeping baby to Pippa. Then, careful to stay several yards behind the man, Kimo and Kim followed him along the side of the greenhouse and around to the clearing where they had long ago dropped off Leaf. They were hoping to see the man get in his car and leave, but instead he went past the Moon Ear Tation sign, up the front steps of the research station, and into the building. With a loud *thwack*, the screen door swung shut behind him.

They stood there wondering what to do next. Should they find out where Johnny's henchman had gone or should they use this opportunity to go back to the greenhouse and put their plan into action? Almost as if in answer to the thought, they heard a huge burst of laughter from around the building. Kimo gestured to Kim that they should go and take a look. She nodded in agreement, and they began to stealthily make their way around the building to the source of the laughter.

As they walked, the laughter got louder and soon they found themselves outside the window of the kitchen. Inside they could see that Johnny's henchman was seated at a table and beside him were Johnny Trout himself and Professor Mumby. The three were all eating large bowls of meatballs, and Johnny was making the other two laugh by tossing the meatballs in the air. Kim and Kimo watched as Wendell, the pig, leapt after the meatballs. It was absolutely mesmerizing; no matter how high or how far Johnny tossed a meatball, the pig was able to snatch it from the air. Sometimes Johnny threw two meatballs at once, but the pig still got them both. Not a single meatball landed on the floor. "Good boy, Wendell," Johnny proclaimed each time the pig did his trick, and each time Kimo felt a little pain in his chest where his heart was. It wasn't easy for the boy to watch his father praise the pig.

Kim sensed this, and she squeezed Kimo's arm in solidarity, even as Professor Mumby was calling out, "Do it again, Wendell." The professor was laughing so hard that her head rocked back and forth, making her mane of pale hair tremble. "Do it again, Wendell!" she said. And Wendell did.

When the last meatball was caught, Kim looked at Kimo. Had they missed the chance to put their plan into action? Was the henchman going to get up and head back to the greenhouse? Kimo shook his head, thinking how they had waited in the bunker above the wharf and it had worked. He was sure that it would work this time too.

And he was right, because just at that moment the professor got up and headed across the kitchen. She opened the door of the freezer and pulled out another package of meatballs, then she poured them into a bowl and put the bowl in the microwave. So apparently the game wasn't over; there was going to be a lot more meatball tossing. Now's our chance, thought Kim, and Kimo was thinking the same thing.

Clouds blotted out the moonlight as Kimo hurried back to the greenhouse where Pippa and Toby were waiting with the baby. Kim went down the road to the place in the woods where they had hidden the car. She had brought the flashlight. It wasn't working very well, but when she banged on it the light came on for a second, and she could see a few feet in front of her before it blinked out again. In this way, she was able to slowly retrace her steps to the car.

Once she'd found the car, she got in and turned the key, saying her mantra—*I can, I can, I can*—as if it were a prayer that might start the sputtering engine. It did, and with the headlights off, Kim drove back to the clearing. Then very slowly, so that the tires wouldn't make much noise, she cruised past the research station to the greenhouse. She found, just as she had hoped, that she was able to drive the car right up alongside the greenhouse to the place where the henchman had exited. Toby and Pippa were already there, holding Penny. Kimo was nowhere to be seen.

"It's locked up," Pippa informed Kim as she set the baby down. She showed Kim that there were two doors with handles. The henchman had strung a thick chain around them and locked it with a padlock.

"Where's Kimo?" Kim asked.

"He's gone to find a rock. We're gonna try breaking the greenhouse glass."

Kim got out and went around to the back of the

car. "I'll make room in the trunk for the plants," she said, almost tripping over Penny, who was playing in the dark grass.

Kimo emerged from the woods carrying a rock the size of a microwave. "Biggest one I could find," he gasped as he lumbered to within a foot of the greenhouse. Then he lifted the rock to his waist and heaved it. There was a dull thud as the rock hit its target. He took a step closer and peered at the glass. "Man," he said, "not even a crack." He picked the rock up and tried again, but again, the rock did no damage. He tried a third time. No luck. "It's not gonna work." He shook his head, discouraged. "What are we gonna do? How are we gonna get the plants? They could be back here any second." He sounded rattled.

Kim, who had been bent over, clearing room in the trunk, suddenly emerged, holding something in the air. "Look!"

They turned and in the darkness they could just barely make out the glint of a long object with something metallic at its end. Kim was holding aloft the ax that Leaf had carried the night they'd met her on the road.

"She left it for us," Kimo said.

"So we could get in the greenhouse and destroy the whamacks," Pippa finished his thought.

"She hid it in the trunk," said Toby, in the breathless voice of a true believer. "She wanted us to find it when we needed it."

"When we were ready to make a sacrifice," Kimo chimed in.

They all looked at Kim, who shrugged and said, "Or it's just a coincidence." She was never going to believe they had met a goddess, but she saw no point in arguing. What did it matter whether Leaf was Maha? Whoever she was, she had inspired them to save the island.

Kim handed Kimo the ax, and he stepped back, lifting the ax to swing it like a baseball bat at the glass. But before he could swing, Pippa stopped his arm. "When the glass cracks," she said, "they'll hear you." Kimo looked to Kim, who nodded. Pippa was right. In fact, they were lucky the stone hadn't worked to break the glass. It would have brought Johnny and the professor running too.

"I know what to do," said Pippa. She threaded the ax handle through the loop of chain and showed Kimo how he could brace the blade against the doorframe and pull down on the handle to exert force. "If you pull hard enough, the chain will break," Pippa said. "That's how leverage works."

"Go, Mega Muscles," said Kim. Sure enough, with Pippa's rigging, Kimo was able to break the chain as easily as if it were a candy necklace.

Moments later they were dragging the first whamacks out of the greenhouse and toward the trunk.

The plants were heavy, large, and bushy. As the children dragged them, they were careful to keep them away from their bodies. After all, those plants had been in cages because their thorny leaf-cups would eat anything that was made of flesh. The Fitzgerald-Trouts did not want to lose a finger or a nose.

They managed to hoist the first load of whamacks into the trunk, then they went back into the greenhouse to get more. The second load was harder to fit into the trunk. They found that they had to stack the cumbersome plants on top of one another. Some of the soil was spilled and some of the leaves were crushed, but they didn't care if those whamacks were damaged; their plan was to destroy the deadly plants by throwing them into the volcano on the top of Mount Muldoon. If the plants got damaged on the way, well, that wasn't a bad thing.

But even shoving and pushing and stacking, they were able to fit only four more whamacks into the trunk. What to do with the last three plants that Kimo, Pippa, and Toby were holding? It was decided that they should sit with them on their laps for the drive up to the volcano. They would roll down their windows and try to stick the bushy parts of the plants outside so that their faces—and their noses—would not be so close to the dangerous leaf-cups. It was awkward, and the pots were very heavy, but they had no other choice. They knew they had to get all the plants into the car for this trip. It was too risky to come back to the research station for a second load.

Kim reached down to grab Penny, who'd been crawling in the grass outside the greenhouse, and she found the baby rolling around in the dark playing with something. Must be her octopus, thought Kim, taking hold of the baby even as she was remembering having left the octopus in the car seat. And that was when Kim saw that Penny was holding on to something alive—and furry. The creature looked terrified. Its ears were standing straight up in the air and its whole body was trembling. They all leaned in to get a closer look.

"It's a jabberwill," said Kimo. "Look at those teeth." So Leaf had been right; the jabberwill was harmless.

Kim was trying to pry the animal out of Penny's clutches. "You have to let it go," she said, gently pulling the animal away. "Now," Kim said firmly, leaning down and looking Penny straight in the eye. "Hurry." The baby seemed to understand. Her lip quivered, but she did not cry as she let go of the creature, which scuttled off into the darkness.

Kim strapped the baby into the car seat while the others, straining to hold the heavy whamacks away from themselves, slid into their seats and poked the bushy parts of the plants out the windows. Kim got behind the steering wheel and turned the key.

The engine sputtered and rumbled and... died. "No," Kim said, banging on the steering wheel, "no, no, no." After so many reliable miles how could the little green car's engine choose *this* moment not to start? Kim closed her eyes, saying her prayer again: *I can, I can, I can.* She turned the key one more time.

Sputter, sputter, rumble, vrooom—the engine came to life. They all breathed a sigh of relief, and Kim slowly pressed on the gas pedal. She drove the length of the greenhouse and was just turning the corner into the clearing when the moon broke through the clouds. Suddenly, there in front of them was Wendell. Johnny had let the pig out of the research building, and he was scratching himself against the Moon Ear Tation sign.

"Duck," said Kimo, sliding down in his seat.

"It's not a duck," said Toby, "it's a pig."

"I meant *duck*, like get down low," Kimo yelped as the car rolled past the pig, but it was too late. Wendell had his head up and was sniffing. The pig had caught a familiar scent, and the scent was *them*.

"*Hrrk-hrrk-hrrk.*" A loud sound came out of Wendell's mouth that was part bark, part snarl, part yelp. "*Hrrk-hrrk-hrrk!*"

"Hit the gas!" Kimo shouted at Kim. There was no point in being quiet now. Kim did as she was told, flicking on the headlights at the same time. The little green car lurched forward past the research station just as Johnny Trout, who had heard Wendell's cry, came running out. What Johnny must have seen, as he barreled down the stairs, was his pig biting at the tires of a car that looked confusingly like a bush because of all those whamacks sticking out its windows.

The bush-car spun out in the gravel right in front of Johnny as Kim tried to get control of the steering wheel. Johnny saw his opportunity and lunged toward the handle of the car door. But he could not find it; it was covered by whamack branches. "Ouch!" he cried, snatching back a finger that must have touched one of the dangerous leaves.

Kim straightened the tires under the car and aimed for the road, pushing down on the gas. The little bush-car sped off. In the rearview mirror, Kim could see Johnny running after them, poking a finger into the air and shouting, "Rotten kids, get back here!" After a moment he gave up and raced in the direction of his truck instead, calling for Wendell, who was close on his heels.

Kim tore down the dirt road, driving more recklessly than she had ever driven before. She had to; the safety of the island depended on the little green car making it to the volcano before Johnny Trout overtook them. They reached the main road, and with a squeal she turned the car onto it. They were headed up on the same road they had driven down when they'd given Leaf a ride. It seemed to Kim that that ride had happened years and years ago, practically in another lifetime. But in fact, it had been only a couple of weeks. There was still so much summer ahead of them.

It was a steep road, and the engine made ominous sounds as it struggled slowly upward. *I can, I can, I can*, Kim told herself, as if by sheer force of will she might keep that engine going to the top of the mountain.

"I think we lost him," said Kimo, who had his eyes trained on the rearview mirror.

"So many bushes, we can't be sure," said Pippa. She was in agony with the heavy whamack on her lap; one of the branches had knocked her glasses askew so she couldn't see properly, but now was not the time for complaints. Besides, she knew if it was hurting her, it must be even worse for Toby, and he wasn't complaining.

"We gotta do something to make sure he can't follow us," said Kimo, and he reached across the steering wheel and snapped off the car's headlights.

"But that's dangerous," said Kim, "not to mention illegal."

"We don't have a choice," Kimo countered. "We're saving the island."

"Right," said Kim just as they reached the turnoff to Muldoon Crater. As she took the turn they all fell silent, sensing how close they were to the end of their mission. If they could just get to the volcano and throw the plants into the lava, they would have done everything they'd set out to do.

"You guys ready?" Kim asked.

"Right-o," said Kimo in his phony British accent. He was trying to seem calm.

"These whamacks aren't gonna know what hit them," snarled Pippa.

"Wait," said Toby, "what's the plan again?" The boy had, as usual, been daydreaming.

Kim took a deep breath. "The minute I park," she explained with all the patience she could muster, "you run to the crater and throw your whamack into the lava. Then you run back and grab another plant from the car and do the same thing."

"Got it," said Toby, then he looked up toward

the sky and added proudly, "I hope Maha's watching."

A moment later, they pulled into the big empty parking lot where tourists parked when they came to take photographs at the rim of the volcano. The parking lot was illuminated by a few streetlamps, though they were entirely unnecessary; the moon shone so brightly over the vast wide-open space, it almost seemed to Kim as if they were in broad daylight. She drove to the edge of the lot, stopping the car as close to the crater as she could. Kimo, Pippa, and Toby swung their doors open and staggered from the car carrying the first three whamacks. They stumbled the long distance across the wide walking path that hugged the crater's rim. Kimo made it to the edge first; Pippa, a few seconds later. The girl peered over and got a shock. "There's no lava!"

It was true. The crater was not full of bubbling lava, as they had expected. The lava was only at the very center of the volcano, and much, much farther away than any of them could throw. Below them, the part of the crater they could reach was full of ash and coals smoldering with heat, like the edges of a monumental campfire.

"Throw it in anyway," said Kimo. "It's hot down there. I bet it'll work." So they did. They tossed the whamacks over the rim and watched as they landed. The plants sat there for a few seconds, then suddenly turned bright red and—*poof!*—collapsed into a pile of ash. So Kimo had been right.

Toby was just struggling up to the crater's rim. His plant was so heavy that the little boy had to drag it. Kimo took it out of his hands and heaved it into the air. They watched it land and sit for a long time. It was nearer to the edge of the crater, where the ash was much less hot. They waited; they watched; they held their breath. At last—*poof!*— the whamack turned red and crumbled into ash.

They all ran back to the car to get another load. Kim was there, lifting the rest of the heavy whamacks from the trunk and lowering them onto the asphalt. She was talking to Penny, who was still strapped into her car seat. "We'll be right back," she said, handing the baby a cookie and making sure Penny's octopus was tucked in beside her.

"Ow ho, ow ho," the baby gurgled enthusiastically.

Kimo, Pippa, and Toby each grabbed another whamack, and this time Kim took one too. They hurried as fast as they could with their heavy loads to the volcano's rim. Out of breath and exhausted, they hurled those four bushes in. They were just turning back for the next load when they heard a familiar buzzing in the sky above them. It was Professor Mumby's copter, hovering overhead.

"She followed us," said Kim.

"She's got a camera," said Pippa. "That means she knows where we are."

"She's probably on the phone to Johnny Trout right now," said Kimo. So there was no time to lose. They hustled back to the car and grabbed four more whamacks.

Now there was only one remaining. Kim, Pippa, and Toby left it there and wearily headed back to the volcano, limping along, dragging their last loads. But Mega Muscles was determined to get the final whamack on this trip too. He would carry one plant in each hand if he had to. He knelt down to grab the second pot and he felt the branches of the whamack that he was already holding brush against his back pocket. He shuddered to think of the leaf-cups touching him, but he mustered his courage and carried on.

It took all the strength he had, but he managed to grip one pot in each hand and was just standing up when he saw headlights coming toward him. Johnny Trout's truck was pulling into the parking lot. So the professor had told him their location, and Johnny was here to stop them.

I won't let him, Kimo thought, stumbling toward the crater. It was a heavy burden that he carried, but he kept on even as Johnny's truck screeched to a stop and Johnny and Wendell leapt out. Sweat was dripping into Kimo's eyes as he chugged the last few feet to the crater's rim, where he could see his siblings waiting. They were shouting, "Hurry! Hurry!" Johnny and Wendell were close on his heels, but Kimo didn't dare turn around.

From where Kim, Pippa, and Toby stood, they could see that Wendell was almost on top of Kimo, but that Johnny had stopped next to the little green car and was bending down to pick something up. There was no time to wonder what it was because the pig was nearly on top of Kimo.

"Hurry!" they shouted again, and Kimo knew that he must reach down inside himself and find his last shred of energy if he was going to save the island. He lifted the whamacks in the air where the pig could not pounce on them, then he picked up his heels and sprinted the final feet to the lip of the crater. He skidded to a stop and heroically heaved the last two whamacks into the air.

They sailed over the crater and flew so far they almost landed in the lava. An instant later, they crumbled into ash. By then, the pig was already leaping onto Kimo's back and knocking him to the ground. Kimo felt the pig's teeth tearing at his clothes, yanking this way and that. It would be only a second until he felt those teeth tearing his flesh. But then something strange happened.

Pippa ran toward the pig. Like all of them, she was afraid of Wendell and his long, sharp teeth, but her rage at the thought of the pig hurting Kimo overtook her. Freckles flaring, she shouted at the creature, "Get off! Get off him!" When the pig didn't stop, Pippa grabbed him by the neck and yanked him backward. "How dare you," she said, whacking him across the snout with her open hand. That did the trick. The pig let out a frightened whimper, unclenched his jaw, and let go of Kimo.

"He's nothing but a coward," said Pippa. She was talking to Johnny Trout, who had just appeared. Kim and Toby helped Kimo to his feet. Kimo shook himself off, straightened his T-shirt, and noticed that he still seemed to be in one piece.

"You don't know him," said Johnny with a shrug. "He's a good pig."

"We know you," said Kimo, feeling the depth of his hurt and resentment toward his father. "We know what a villain you are. How could you bring those plants here, knowing what they would do? How could you get rich by killing our home?"

"What are you talking about?" Johnny was kneeling down and stroking the pig, looking at Kimo, genuinely mystified.

"The notebook," said Kimo, "we found it."

"Oh, that," said Johnny with a chuckle. "Those articles and notes. That's all a load of bunk. Scientists have been saying that kind of thing about whamacks for years. But no one has real proof. I'm collecting those notes and articles so I can draft a paper of my own. Here's what I know. People like to get worked up, but these things—knockabouts, floods, volcanoes—they go in cycles. Sometimes there are more of them and sometimes there aren't.

The weather has a way of working itself out. And in the meantime, I need to make a living. Poor Wendell's got to eat." He looked over at the pig with all the affection he didn't feel for his son.

"I don't believe you," said Kimo. "The island is sick, and you've made it that way." Then Kimo did a very strange thing. Something that his brother and sisters said later they weren't sure he should have done. Kimo looked his father square in the eye and said, "If you promise never to bring another shipment of whamacks to the island, I'll give you the boat."

Kim started to say something, but Kimo silenced her with a look. Johnny Trout laughed and said, "You'll give me the boat?"

"I will," said Kimo, "but you've got to do something you've probably never done before—you've got to promise no more whamacks, and you've got to keep your word." Kimo was hoping there was one shred of decency in his father and that he could get him to dig down and find it.

"I'm not gonna make that promise," said Johnny with another laugh. Then the old pirate stood up and tugged on his whiskered chin. "You really have got yourself worked up about these whamacks. You shouldn't bother, you know? They've been banned for export from Oceania. I couldn't get another shipment if I wanted to. Whamacks have a short life. That's why this was such a good business. Everyone who bought a plant always needed another plant eventually. But this shipment was special. I was going to use some of the plants to breed more, right here on this island. You put an end to that, didn't you?" Kimo couldn't help but smile. Johnny, however, wasn't smiling. "As for your boat," he said, scratching his stubbly face, "I don't think you ever owned it."

Kimo raised an eyebrow, perplexed, and now Johnny did smile, reaching into his pocket and pulling out the thing he had picked up from the ground beside the little green car. It was the piece of paper that proclaimed Kimo Fitzgerald-Trout the owner of Grimstone Fishing Vessel Serial Number 78d2b. The deed to the boat.

When Kimo had bent down to pick up the final whamack, the plant he was holding had brushed against his back pocket and the deed had fallen out. (Later, when the children recounted the story, they would all say it was as if the whamack had sensed what was coming—its smoldering death in the volcano—and one of those carnivorous pickpocketing plants had reached into Kimo's back pocket and lifted the deed out, thereby exacting its revenge.)

However it had gotten there, Johnny was, indeed, holding the deed. He waved it back and forth, taunting Kimo. "I always planned to keep the boat," he said, "but your little game here, destroying my whamacks, well, let's just say it hasn't made me want to change my mind. So here's what's going to happen. I'm gonna do to this piece of paper what you just did to my investment. I'm going to throw it in the volcano so that no one will ever know it was your boat."

Kimo shot back at his father, "Captain Grimstone knows." He was putting on a brave face.

"Captain Grimstone is the man who let me drive away with the boat in the first place." Johnny shrugged. The children knew he spoke the truth. No grown-up was going to believe that the boat was theirs when another grown-up said it wasn't.

And Johnny knew that they knew.

He gave them another big, snaggletoothed smile, then he rolled up the deed and took a step closer to the crater. Kimo tried to get in his way, he tried to snatch at the paper, but Johnny was too quick for him. He tossed the deed up over Kimo's head.

The children watched as it flew end over end through the air and into the volcano. Then they cast down their eyes. The boat was lost to them forever.

Or was it?

Because as soon as the paper left Johnny's hand,

good old Wendell, well-trained, obedient Wendell, did something marvelous. He must have thought the deed flying through the air was yet another game of fetch because he took off after it like it was one of those meatballs, and as the deed sailed over the edge of the crater, so did Wendell.

Johnny saw what was happening, and he whistled his whistle to call the pig back, but it was too late. The pig could not turn back. He was already in midair.

He fell through the sky and landed in the volcano with a yowl so loud it made the whole mountain shake. Poor Johnny couldn't stand it. The second he heard his beloved pig in pain, he went crazy. He had to do something. So he made a sacrifice of his own. He leapt over the edge of the crater after his pet.

The Fitzgerald-Trouts rushed to the rim and stared down at the spot where the deed to the boat had landed and burned, the spot where Johnny and Wendell were now dancing in the hot ash, turning to run together back to the crater's rim.

The children looked at one another and shook their heads; there was no going after the pair. Instead they ran back to the parking lot to find Johnny's cell phone in his truck so that they could call an ambulance.

As they ran, they could all hear the shouts of the man and the pig echoing off the crater walls. Pippa summed it up. "Horrible," she said. "I'm glad Penny didn't see that."

CHAPTER
19

On a bright sunny day a few weeks later, the
children had the boat anchored off Skoot's
Point and were enjoying a big bag of doughnuts
that Mr. Knuckles and Asha had brought them.
They had counted the doughnuts and divided
them up, and now they each had five doughnuts piled in their laps. Kim was eating bites of
doughnut and looking up at the cliff where only a
few weeks before they had watched lava pouring
into the sea. The road that ran alongside the cliff

was still impassable, covered as it was by the black volcanic stone, and Kim was thinking how wonderful it was that it didn't matter to them. They didn't need to be on that road. They were living on a boat.

"Is there anything better than a doughnut?" asked Pippa, who was licking the icing from hers.

"Not when you're eating a doughnut," said Kimo.

"They taste fresh," said Pippa. "I think Asha actually paid for these."

"It must be true love," said Kim.

Mr. Knuckles and Asha had taken to bringing the children doughnuts whenever they saw the boat docked at the wharf. They felt they owed the children something for their help in getting them back together. It happened like this.

A few days after the Night of the Burning Whamacks (as the children had taken to calling it), they had gone to the laundromat to do their laundry and had discovered that the place was still closed. "This is getting ridiculous," Pippa had said, and without consulting the others, she had marched around to the back of the building, climbed the stairs, and knocked on the door. When Mr. Knuckles opened it, Pippa grabbed him by the arm and dragged him outside, telling him that he was going to the grocery store to talk to Asha. Mr. Knuckles had resisted, saying, "She not want talk. She not like me."

"That's not true," said Pippa. "She thinks you're terrific."

"Then why she not come here?" Mr. Knuckles moaned, and Pippa realized he was resisting talking to Asha because he was scared of being rejected. But Pippa—who had faced down the pig, Wendell—knew how good it could feel to be brave. "If Asha is important to you, you've got to risk going there and facing her."

And Kim, who had by then climbed the stairs to join her sister, offered, "You can't lie here in the dark wishing she loved you. You have to try."

In the end, Mr. Knuckles had agreed to go, and

the group of them had walked across the parking lot to the grocery store. He'd had a moment of hesitation when he walked through the doors. "What if she with frozen food manager?"

"Then you say good-bye and go," said Toby, who was having trouble understanding—or caring about—the twists and turns of Mr. Knuckles's romantic life.

They found Asha at the back of the store, elbow-deep in an enormous bowl of coleslaw. She looked up as they came through the door, and she locked eyes with Mr. Knuckles. Her lip began to quiver as if she were going to cry. "I suppose congratulations are in order," she said. She had stopped stirring the coleslaw.

Mr. Knuckles shook his head and said, "What?"

"Your wedding," Asha replied, blinking back a tear.

"Wedding?"

Now it was Asha's turn to look confused. "You married the lucky lady."

Mr. Knuckles hesitated, then he overcame his fear and nervously said, "You the only lady for me, Asha." They all held their breath as they waited to see how she would respond.

"I am?" An enormous smile broke across Asha's face. "Oh, Hurley," she said, and the Fitzgerald-Trouts had to plug their ears. Hearing the two grown-ups say each other's first names was way too embarrassing.

It quickly became clear that their breakup had been a terrible misunderstanding. It turned out that Mr. Knuckles had been so nervous about asking Asha to marry him that he had written down exactly what he was going to say to her, but Asha had found the piece of paper with the writing on it and had thought it was a love letter to someone else. She was furious and heartbroken—or, as Kimo had put it, "chewed up and spit out like a buggy hammock." (They had all decided that Toby's version of the lyrics made as much sense as any of the others.) That was why Asha had told Mr. Knuckles the lie that she had a date with the frozen food manager.

When she realized the mistake she'd made, Asha gave a yelp of happiness and ran to Mr. Knuckles, hugging him and getting coleslaw from her hands all over the back of his tank top. But Mr. Knuckles didn't care. "Marry me," he said, and Asha nodded. Later that afternoon, they'd hopped on his motorcycle and driven to the courthouse, and he had slid the metal detector ring with the little green stone onto Asha's finger.

Just before they'd left, the children had told Asha the part that she had played in helping them find their boat by telling them about the purchase of Blue Miracle Sunshine Food. Asha was delighted by her role, and explained to them that she had also found out something about the professor. "She's not a real scientist," she told them. "I found out she had her first name legally changed to Professor so that she would sound like she was."

"That's the weirdest thing I've ever heard," said Pippa.

"Tell me about it," said Asha. "Like if I changed my first name to Doctor and then tried to perform brain surgery."

"I wouldn't let you near my head," said Toby. This made Pippa rush over to him and wiggle her fingers on his scalp, pretending to do brain surgery. Toby played it up, rolling his eyes and sticking out his tongue and acting like Pippa's surgery had made him sick. Their pantomime made Asha laugh her magical laugh that sounded like waves sloshing over pebbles, and that made everyone else laugh too.

Now they were anchored at Skoot's Point and eating Asha's doughnuts with gusto. Toby was holding Goldie's jar and showing the goldfish that he could fit two into his mouth at once; Kimo was spinning one around his finger like a Hula-Hoop; Pippa was taking bites of hers from the middle out;

and Kim had already finished all five and was feeding Penny, who was pretending to feed her stuffed octopus but was actually just mushing doughnut onto the animal's face. Between bites the baby would say her new favorite word: "Terri-bull, terri-bull, terri-bull."

Since the Night of the Burning Whamacks, the baby said the word every time Johnny Trout's name was mentioned. And his name was mentioned a lot.

How could they not talk about the excitement of seeing Johnny and Wendell hoisted by emergency helicopter from the smoldering crater of the volcano? How could they not describe—over and over—their horrified awe as they watched the helicopter fly off above the treetops with the man and the pig dangling from wires that stretched a hundred feet below its belly? How could they not turn to one another a dozen times a day and scrunch up their faces in a snaggletoothed grin and say "So here's what's going to happen" just the way

Johnny Trout had said it? How could they not point their fingers in the air and wave their fists and shout "Rotten kids, you oughta mind your own business"—which was a line they loved precisely because it mixed what Johnny had said to them with what the villain had said to the nosy ninja? How could they not repeat Johnny's words about Kimo never having owned the boat when they themselves were running up and down the boat's deck or jumping from its bow or pressing its throttle full speed ahead? How could they not?

They knew from island rumor that Johnny and Wendell had been safely delivered to the hospital, where they were soaked in tubs of cooling medicine, then wrapped in bandages from head to foot. Rumor also had it that Wendell's tail was so badly scorched the whole hospital smelled like bacon. There were further rumors that Johnny had agreed to pay whatever it cost to get first-class medical treatment for his beloved pet, who was placed in a hospital bed right beside his owner.

Only weeks before, Kimo would have been angry to hear about Wendell being treated so well by Johnny, when Kimo himself had been treated so badly. But strangely, the encounter with his father on the mountain had changed all that. Now Kimo felt glad that even though his father was terrible in some ways, at least he wasn't terrible in all ways. At least Johnny Trout loved *something*, even if that something wasn't Kimo.

The others didn't agree. "Terri-bull, terri-bull, terri-bull," Penny chanted between bites of dough-nut, and as far as the others were concerned, Penny was right. After all, from his hospital bed Johnny Trout had hired lawyers and begun legal pro-ceedings against the five Fitzgerald-Trout chil-dren. It was his assertion that Grimstone Fishing Vessel Serial Number 78d2b was his, and that the children—who he had heard were driving around in it—were committing theft.

The Fitzgerald-Trouts would recount these facts to one another and then shrug and laugh and say, "But if he owns it, how come we're living on it?" Kim hoped the judge and the jury would say the same thing. But she could not let herself worry about it too much. In fact, the number one thing on her (mental) to-do list was *Try not to worry so much.*

She lay back on the deck and let Penny pull herself to her feet holding on to the boat's rail. Every day the baby got closer to walking. In the meantime she crawled around the boat wearing a life jacket that Pippa had fashioned by duct-taping empty Uncle Ozo's bottles to a onesie. That had been on Kim's to-do list too: *Get Penny a life jacket,* and then one day Pippa had done it without being asked. Pippa wasn't happy with the design. She thought the bottles were too cumbersome, and she was still experimenting with other things that could be used to make the baby float, but so far she hadn't found anything as good as the plastic bottles. To Kim, it seemed like a good invention, and it had reminded her that sometimes she could count on her siblings to help with the things that needed to be done.

Thinking of the to-do list made Kim think about other things on it, and so she said, "Toby, can you please name the continents?"

Toby scratched his head and looked at his beloved goldfish, then looked out across the water where, he remembered, those whamacks had come from. "Oceania?" he tried.

"It's not officially a continent," said Kim, thinking to herself, Well, it's a start.

She was about to say so to Toby when they heard an enormous racket coming from the cliffs. They turned away from the water and back to the land, where they saw the branches of the trees shaking as thousands and thousands of birds took to the air. Kim remembered what Leaf had said that night in the car, and over the noise of the birds, she shouted, "Something big is coming."

"Sure is," Kimo yelled. He was pointing to the water, where there was a curious sight. The waves that usually traveled across the ocean and crashed up against the cliffs had now reversed themselves. They were coming *from* the island out to the ocean.

"Interesting," said Kimo, who felt no fear of the waves. "The island must be shaking against the water." Even as he said this, they felt a series of tremors. Next came a noise so monumental it was as if a trash compactor the size of the island were suddenly grinding to life.

But it wasn't a trash compactor; it was the volcano.

They could now see—miles away from them—an enormous cloud of smoke and ash rising out of Mount Muldoon. They watched the cloud, and they held their breath, and a second later, out of the middle of that cloud, appeared a spout of fiery lava. It shot straight up into the air, hundreds of feet, before it fell back down to earth, pouring its hot, liquid rock over the mountain.

At the same time, a cloud of ash and smoke was spreading, like spilled ink, across the blue sky. It poured into the sky above the island and then above the ocean and then above the Fitzgerald-Trouts.

They tilted their heads back and stared at the ominous black cloud. None of them spoke, but when they talked about it later, they all said they were thinking the same thing: They didn't feel afraid. They somehow knew, deep in their bones, that whatever was happening wasn't going to hurt them or anyone else.

That is what they were thinking as they stood with their faces upturned and saw the black cloud open and a great gray mass begin to fall toward them.

"Cover your heads!" Kimo shouted, because he had realized it wasn't rainfall. It was *rock*fall.

Plop, a rock fell.

And then, *plop*, another rock.

Plop. Plop. Plop.

Another, and another, and another.

There were rocks falling all over them, but amazingly the rocks didn't hurt. They hardly felt like anything at all. In fact, the rocks weren't rocks. They were more like gray sponges and they were as light as the marshmallows that grew on the trees in Tobyworld. They were the kind of thing, Kim said later, that a mouse might use as a pillow. "Pumice," said Kimo, who had been taught about such things. And so it was.

The pumice fell all over them, all over the boat, all over the ocean. It piled up in huge drifts on the deck, and for as far as their eyes could see; looking out over the railing of the boat, there were pumice stones on top of the water like croutons floating on a bowl of soup.

"Hey," said Pippa, picking up one of the spongy blobs and testing how light it was. "If it floats, I can use it for Penny's life jacket." She grinned at Kim, pleased with her invention. Kim smiled back. She was thinking about how amazing the island was. Right now it was spewing hot lava that would make the island grow bigger and stronger. And even as it was doing that—healing itself—it was also bringing them magical floating stones. Kimo had been right. More than the boat or the car or anyplace else, the island was their home. It had always taken care of them, and if they took care of it, it always would.

Kim picked up a piece of pumice and threw it at Kimo. He grabbed one and threw it at her. Then Toby got in on it, and Pippa, and the baby. They threw the spongy blobs at one another and they ran and slid and dodged and jumped. All the rumbling sounds of the island had faded, and the air around them was filled with laughter.

ACKNOWLEDGMENTS

My great thanks to the five Fitzgerald-Trout children, who trusted me to tell their story. Thank you also to the others who gave me their versions of these events, especially Hurley Knuckles, Asha Kosmo, and Clayton Grimstone. Thanks to my pugnacious legal team at Bumbleman, Trotter & Gulch, who supported the publication of this book despite legal threats from Johnny Trout.

I had many readers, young and otherwise, whose comments were invaluable. Thank you to Semi Chellas, Rory Evans, Douglas Fudge, Gemma Fudge, Jozy Harris, Silas Harris, Hilary Liftin, Finnegan Sanders, Graley Sanders, Kristin Sanders, Evan Savian, and Linda Spalding. Thanks to Sam Goldbach, whose imagination inspired me. Thanks to my marvelous and very patient agent, Jackie Kaiser. To Jerry Kalajian, who believed in these books from the beginning. To the Tundra team, especially Tara Walker and Vikki Van Sickle. To everyone at Little, Brown, especially Jenny Choy, Nikki Garcia, Sasha Illingworth, and Jessica Shoffel.

I owe more than thanks to the incomparable and extraordinary Susan Rich, who if she ever runs for mayor of our island will get my vote, and to Sydney Smith, who continues to draw the island and its inhabitants with great panache; I feel beyond lucky to work with both of them.

Finally, thanks to Mrs. Annetta Kinnicutt, who shared with me (and with so many island children) her love of books.

Esta Spalding grew up on a tropical island where she never wore shoes. She has since lived all over the world. When she's not writing, she kayaks, bakes, and assembles whale skeletons with her husband, a marine biologist. She invites you to find out more at estaspalding.com.

Sydney Smith spent his childhood as a naturalist and researcher in rural Nova Scotia, where he paid close attention to wild creatures and things that grow in dirt. His interests led him to art school. He has since illustrated many extraordinary books, including Jon Arno Lawson's *Sidewalk Flowers*.